D0305588

# ALBERT'S MEMORIAL

# ALBERT'S MEMORIAL

a novel by

## David Cook

An Alison Press Book

Secker & Warburg · London

First published in England 1972 by
The Alison Press/Martin Secker & Warburg Limited
14 Carlisle Street, London W1V 6NN

SBN 436 10670 1

YF 1/75

Printed by Northumberland Press Limited
Gateshead

For John Bowen

# CONTENTS

## *Part One*

### MARY

## *Part Two*

### PAUL

# Part Three

## PAUL AND MARY

# PART ONE

# MARY

# BRING YOUR LOVE TO JESUS

'Don't want any of those chubby cherubs, girl. No, I don't want a stone of any kind. No, not even one of those nice black marble ones with my name on it. You can get me one of those square vases, and put my name on that, so that nobody will be tempted to pinch it.'

Even though Albert had joked about death and told her his wishes, Mary had never entertained the possibility of his going first. They had often spent sunny Sunday afternoons laughing at the chubby cherubs, or trying to beat one another in finding the oldest or the newest gravestone in Kensal Green Cemetery.

Now Mary was standing beside the newest. It wasn't a gravestone. It was a square black marble vase, with 'ALBERT GEOFFREY WATSON, 1917-1969, NOT FORGOTTEN' engraved in gold leaf.

He had been dead four days.

Mary and the vicar stood facing each other over the grave. There had been no one else to ask. Neither Albert nor she had any relatives that she knew of. She was forced, she thought, to wear something black, so she had bought a hat. It didn't suit her, but there was little choice in black. One would have thought that there were enough funerals to make black a popular colour.

The vicar had chosen the best side of the grave for reading, his back to the sun. Everything seemed unreal. Mary watched a tuft of unruly grey hair on the vicar's crown, backlit by the sun and glittering, wave from side to side. She made it out to be a fairy standing on top of his head, and waving her wand to open the coffin for Albert to rise and swear at the chubby cherubs.

'You must cultivate a hobby. Come to church, Mary. Find God again. We have many widows in the parish who find relief and satisfaction in His company.'

They were walking back to the gate. Mary was between the vicar and the sun. For the first time, she saw his face properly. Hairs stuck out of his ears. His eyes were tired; they looked at everything except her.

'I hope you're not going home to brood. I should be very displeased, Mary, to think that. Death is to be rejoiced in. Alfred, I'm sure, was a good man. He will wait for you in heaven, I have no doubt.'

'Albert.'

'Yes, of course; Albert. I'm not very good on names. That's why I do more deaths than christenings.'

He had made a joke, and he smiled to prove it. The vicar opened the gate, and Mary passed through it into the Harrow Road.

'I'm sure Albert will be kept alive in your thoughts. Memories can be a great comfort, if we use them properly. Goodbye, Mary, and don't forget to bring your love to Jesus.'

It was a Thursday and the shops were closed, otherwise she would have bought herself a cake for tea. There was brown bread back at the flat. She would make some toast, and have jam on it.

She wouldn't wear the hat again; it didn't suit her. It had a large brim, and made her feel like a schoolgirl.

'Half an ounce of Condor Sliced, please.' Mary had entered the only shop open in the street.

'Very nice too; I smoke it myself. There we are, four and

twopence. Wish I could get my wife to smoke a pipe instead of chewing it.' The man laughed.

'No, it's not for me. It's for . . .'

The man took her money, and closed the till. Mary stood holding the tobacco. The distance between her and the counter seemed to have widened. The man was moving to the back of the shop.

'Will you take it back, please? He's dead. He died four days ago; he can't smoke it.'

Taking off the hat (she wouldn't wear it any more), Mary put the kettle on. When they had come to take him away, they had wanted to remake the bed and change the sheets. Mary had stopped them. It was an old mattress, and since Albert always slept on the same side, the mark his body had made was still in the bed.

Mary knelt down, and placed her head in the hollow made by Albert's buttocks, but the smell of him had gone. From the bottom drawer of the dresser, where she had hidden them, she took the last pair of underpants he had worn. Laying them carefully in the hollow, she knelt down again, and covered them with her face.

The kettle whistled, but Mary stayed with her head on one side, her hand tracing the outline of Albert's legs.

The kettle boiled dry almost at the same time as the gas ran out. Mary pulled herself up, and had to sit on the bed for a moment until her leg, which had gone to sleep, woke up and allowed her to walk on it. A shilling was taken from the cup in which they always kept shillings, a shilling that Albert might have put there. Mary looked into the cup, and picked a very worn shilling, which she knew that she herself had saved.

The gas came hissing out of the little black holes, making a comforting sound. Mary looked down at the greasy gas-ring, and listened to it. The smell became sickening, and frightened her, so she turned it off.

Drinking milk from Albert's china mug, and eating a slice of brown bread and marmalade, Mary contemplated life without him. She had no friends. With Albert, she needed none. They had lived together for over twenty years without the need of friends. Albert knew the people he worked with, and went to the pub three nights a week to play dominoes. The rest of the time, they watched television.

Mary switched on the television, and saw a children's programme on how to make a spacesuit with brown paper.

At six fifteen, which was the time Albert got home from work, Mary opened the door of their flat, and looked down the stairs. Five minutes later, she went down the stairs, opened the front door, and stood on the step, one foot still in the doorway to prevent its closing.

Mary stood, and then sat on the doorstep until it grew dark. The old man who lived alone across the hall came home from work, and said 'Good evening', which was all he ever said. And the two girls who lived on the ground floor asked if she was all right. Mary told them that she was getting some fresh air, and one of them replied that it was indeed fresh, and tugged at her cardigan.

They knew that she was looking for Albert, and that he was dead. They had been there when the policeman had come to see her, and later they had seen the undertaker call, and they had given her a bunch of irises from their garden to take with her to the funeral. But she had once overheard one of them say that Albert was a grumpy old sod, so she had put the flowers on someone else's grave.

When it became too cold to sit on the doorstep any longer, Mary went upstairs for her keys. She went through the flat, opening every door just in case. Despite the fact that all Albert's clothes, save the ones she had seen him buried in, were in the wardrobe, Mary closed the door of the flat, and walked down the road to the pub he used.

Christmas was the only time she had ever been there. For the last nine Christmases, she and Albert had sat where she was sitting now, she drinking shandy and he bitter, singing carols with the regulars.

Mary sipped the shandy she didn't want, and watched three men play dominoes. None of the men knew her well enough to speak to her, and she had no wish to talk to them. From time to time, one of them would glance round at her, as if he should know her but didn't.

She kept half of her shandy until 'Last Orders', and then stood.

'Aren't you going to finish your drink, mum?'

Mary turned to the young Irish barman. 'No, he'll be at home.'

She knew he was dead. She had buried him. Thrown earth on top of the coffin. Talked to the vicar about remembering him. The vicar had said that memories could be a comfort if used properly. What did he mean by 'properly'? 'Use your memories properly.'

He was not waiting in the flat because he was dead. He had not been playing dominoes in the pub because he was dead. He hadn't walked down the street at six fifteen, or opened the door with his key, or put his lunch-bag on the kitchen table, or looked inside the pans on the stove, or switched on the radio, or sat across from her with his feet against hers under the table, or said he liked the food and asked for more, or complained about the television programmes and switched them off, or lain in bed waiting while she washed herself twice in the kitchen, or said she smelt of soap. He was not in bed, because he was dead.

Mary lay on her side of the bed, her hand stroking the

15

hollow Albert had left. Her insides longed for him. She could feel herself open and close, waiting for a hand to reach out, waiting for him to roll over with all his weight, and slide in to her, his breath around her face, his sweat sticking to them both. They had not made love every night, or indeed at all. Much. Recently. But she had felt his warmth, and imagined. As long as he was there, she had lain on her back, legs apart, until she had heard him snore. Then she had touched his bottom with her hand, and fallen asleep.

Mary's hand stroked the hollow in the mattress, and her ear listened to the clock's tick.

At four o'clock, the light came through the thin curtains. At six, Mary got up, and dressed.

The Tubes had just started, so Mary took one to Harlesden. Outside John Daniels, Jig and Tool Makers, on the other side of the road, is a bench. Mary sat on the bench until six in the afternoon, and then until fifteen minutes past six when the last man had gone home.

The flat was just as she had left it, but she opened every door just in case. The girls from downstairs had pushed a note under Mary's door to ask if there was anything they could do. Mary murmured 'Use your memories properly,' and went to sit in the pub.

The young barman attempted to involve her in conversation, but quickly saw that she wished to be left alone. At 'Last Orders', Mary went home, but found herself reluctant to get into bed.

At 2 a.m. she fell asleep on the settee, and at six thirty she took the Tube to Harlesden. But at six fifteen in the evening, she did not go home and look for Albert, because Albert was dead. She did, however, go to the cemetery to sit with him.

At the gate of the cemetery, she remembered that, at this time of year, it closed at 6 p.m., and indeed the notice in front of her said so.

In the pub, the three men had found a fourth to play dominoes, and the barman said no more than 'Good evening.'

Again that night, Mary found that she didn't wish to sleep in the bed, or even go into the bedroom. She moved all her clothes out into the living-room, laying them over chairs and on top of the chest of drawers. She didn't sleep much on the settee, but next day she would sit with Albert by his grave, and maybe she would sleep then.

At the end of the week, Mary was left a note to say that the Insurance Man would be calling at a certain time, and would she please make a point of being at home.

Kensal Green Cemetery serves most of West London, and covers approximately eighty-five acres. It is maintained by four or five gardeners. Consequently, a great deal of it is not maintained at all, and has gone to seed. Gravestones lean against one another for support, and long grass and weeds bury those graves which have only small stones or no stone at all.

To the romantic nature, the cemetery might appear romantic. But to anyone about to bury or be buried there, it must cast grave doubts on their hopes of being remembered long in this life. Nevertheless, so many acres of long grass and broken tombstones in the centre of London are beautiful.

The graves were so close together. It made Mary wonder whom Albert was lying next to. The gravestone she was sitting on belonged to a Chinaman. At the foot of the grave was an open book carved in stone, with the Chinaman's photograph on one facing page and a list of the people who would mourn for him on the other. At the other side of Albert, a rough wooden cross with 'My Dear Mother' scribbled childishly on it in pencil marked the head of another new grave, and nine vases of plastic flowers had been arranged on it in threes. One of the vases was a chalk swan with its head and neck broken, and the head had been stuffed in among roses that seemed to be made out of plastic lace. A large plastic daisy formed the centrepiece.

'I always admire black marble, don't you?'

Standing next to Mary on a pair of very thin legs, her bony feet pressed into old casual shoes, was a woman.

'I'll bet you didn't get that for nothing, eh?' Her stockings were wrinkled by the thinness of the legs inside them. One had a large hole which showed a network of blue veins.

'Aren't flowers a price though?' the woman said, as if they had been talking on the subject for hours. Her voice was a croak, as though she had lived a long time with rooks. Mary nodded.

'When you've been coming here thirteen years like me, you'll get used to it.' She wore a shapeless pink suit, and an off-white blouse. Her hands also reminded Mary of large birds. It was not that they looked like birds. It was the way the woman grasped her bunch of seedy wallflowers.

'It's a shame to have a lovely marble vase like that, and no flowers.' The woman's knees cracked, as she bent down and pressed them against Albert's mound of earth. From the bunch of seven or eight stems, she chose two, clipping them short with scissors that hung from her waist on a chain.

'I come here every day if I can. My vase doesn't hold much water, so I have to keep topping it up. This one's nice and big. You won't need to come more than once a week with a vase like this.' The two ludicrously small flowers rolled to one side of the vase, and refused to be separated. The woman fiddled with them as though she were giving a demonstration on television.

'You need a lot for a good showing, but it's a bit of colour, isn't it? Mine's over here.' Her knees cracked again as she stood. For a moment Mary thought the woman's free hand was going to grasp one of hers, and press it like the wallflowers which were visibly wilting.

The woman went ahead, tracking her way through the long grass, and striding over forgotten graves. Suddenly, when Mary thought they were lost, they came to a clearing and a neatly turfed grave, on which sat a cheap glass vase, and in it wallflowers, identical to the ones in the woman's hand. Mary admired two tiny yellow flowers which were growing out of the grave itself.

'One of the young gardeners put those in when he turfed it for me. They all know me here. Thirteen years is a long time. I come here more than anybody. No one could ever have done more.' The woman removed the wallflowers from the vase. They were no more dead than the ones in her hand.

'If she only knew she was here, she'd turn in her grave.'

Mary asked why.

'Too much water about. There's a canal over there, isn't there? Mind you, they need it, with Wormwood Scrubs on the other side.'

Through the overgrown hedge, Mary could just make out a patch of water.

'She always said not to bury her in this cemetery, or she'd die twice. Too much water swells you out, and aids decomposure. That means you rot faster.' As she said this, the woman's eyes filled with water, and her voice lost its croak and became a whisper.

Finally, when the woman had finished, they walked back to one of the avenues between the graves. When they had almost reached the gate, Mary excused herself by saying she wished to go back to Albert's grave. The woman seemed hurt by this, and asked if Mary would not consider a cup of tea at a café round the corner. Mary explained that she had brought a flask. The woman stood still, nodding and repeating the word 'flask'. There then followed a silence, while the woman's thin tight face searched Mary's. After a while, Mary found the words she needed. 'I'm sorry I can't offer you a drink, but I was here early this morning, so most of it is gone.'

Backing away, Mary saw the woman's expression change. Before it had been tense and pinched. Now the muscles relaxed, and the eyes looked tired, as they had for a moment when the woman had said, 'If you bury me here, I'll die twice.'

The following morning, four American tourists, who were early visitors to the cemetery, found Mary creeping out of the tomb of Adrian Stanley Winstanton, in which she had spent the night. The four travellers had paused to read the inscription on the good man's tomb, and to learn that he had been an Importer of Indian and China Teas to the Nobility, 1826 to 1893.

Mary blinked at the daylight, and hobbled away. She had gone to sleep, sitting up in a corner of the tomb, because the floor was too dirty to lie on. The tomb itself was some five feet square and twelve feet high, and she had shared it with a dustbin lid and two sparrows. It had been easy for her to get into the tomb, because the bottom half of the door had been kicked away. Mary had half expected to find a coffin on a slab inside, but when she had crawled out of the rain and into its dark warmth, all she had touched was the dustbin lid.

The position in which she had gone to sleep now caused her a good deal of pain. The stone she had sat on had been small for a seat, and her head had twisted itself in the night, so that one side of her neck now ached for all it was worth. But she was on her way to talk to Albert. Nothing else mattered.

It had happened quite simply. The woman in pink had left, and Mary was sitting on the grave next to Albert's, looking at the black marble vase. She had been there all day, and it was now almost 6 p.m. The lodge-keeper had rung his hand-bell to warn people that he was going to lock the gates, and Mary had woken from a daydream to realize once again where Albert was, and that he would not be going home with her.

'If you've changed your mind about a chubby cherub, I can get you one. The Insurance Man's been, and given me a cheque.'

'I don't want no bloody cherub, girl. What you going to live on, if you spend that?'

It was a reasonable question, and one she had not thought of. It was not until she had considered it for a moment that she realized who had asked it. Thinking she might have misheard, she tried again with something that she knew would provoke a reply.

'I could always get a job.'

'Who, you? Don't be daft. Who'd be silly enough to take you on? They'd have to have their heads seen to.'

She was so excited that she couldn't think of anything else to say. Every time she tried to speak, she laughed so much that the words wouldn't come out. She stood, and moved round the grave trying to control herself, but it was no use. Laughing and crying at the same time, Mary rolled about. The keeper had locked the gates, and gone home. She was alone with Albert, and he was talking to her.

'And take those bloody dog-flowers out of my pot.' The voice didn't come from the grave, but from inside her head. It was Albert's voice, though; there was absolutely no doubt about that. Mary mouthed his words, and knew what he was going to say before he'd finished, but it was Albert's voice and Albert's thoughts and, what's more, it sounded like him.

When she could stop herself laughing, Mary fired a series of questions at Albert, concerning his untimely death, questions which neither the policeman, the doctor, nor the letter from Albert's employers had answered to her satisfaction.

Albert had been on his way back to his workbench after

lunch, when he had fallen, and cut his head open. The factory ambulance had rushed him to the Casualty Department of a local hospital to have it stitched. The hospital had then sent him home with instructions to stay in bed for a week, because he had lost a lot of blood. Albert had stayed in bed three weeks, showing no sign of wanting to get up, or eat, or talk about it. At the end of the fourth week, Mary had come home from shopping, and found him dead. The doctor had signed the death certificate, and said he was sorry, but there was nothing he could do. Albert had just decided to give up the fight.

The main question Mary asked Albert, as she sat above his grave, was why he had given up the fight. But there was no answer, and all she saw was Albert's expression as it had been when he pushed his food away and stared at the wallpaper.

The other question was, how had he tripped. He was not a clumsy man, quite the reverse, careful and methodical. It would be unlike him to stumble. In twenty years, Mary could not remember having seen him fall. There was no question of drink. The letter from his firm had said that: 'We wish to make it clear, Mrs Watson, that there was no question of Albert's being under the influence of drink.' As if they needed to explain that to her! What they hadn't made clear was why he had fallen; nor had the policeman who came to report the accident, and tell her not to worry, nor the doctor who could not tell her why Albert had given up the fight.

'How did you fall, Albert?'

But Albert had just said, 'Leave it alone,' and turned away, to look at the wallpaper.

Now in the cemetery when Mary asked again, she got the same reply, or none at all. Not wishing to antagonize him too much, she changed the subject, and said she missed him, and still loved him. It started to rain, and Albert told her to take cover. She replied that she would talk to him a lot. Water began to collect on the stone where she sat, and Albert told her she would get piles. She replied that she was very happy he'd decided to talk to her. The rain pressed harder, and she felt it soaking through her clothes. Albert told her that if she didn't get out of it soon, he wouldn't say another word. She replied that she hoped he would visit her whenever he could. The cold made her shiver, and caused her teeth to chatter, making further conversation difficult. The rain ran down Mary's face with such force that she found it hard to see. Albert told her that she was a bloody stupid cow. She replied by wishing him a good night, and running to find shelter. As she left, Albert laughed, and told her she would catch her death.

Mary supposed that this was what the vicar had meant when he said 'Use your memories properly, and they'll be a great comfort.' It was a comfort, a great comfort. The morning was cold, but Mary's clothes had dried on her overnight. She had not dared to take them off, for fear of being caught, and charged with nudity as well as trespass. When she got back to Albert's grave, he was very talkative, and said he hoped she had slept well. She told him in whose tomb she had spent the night, and he said he would find out if it was all right.

At nine thirty-five, a thin pink figure could be seen hurrying through the cemetery gates, looking from right to left. The figure disappeared into the long grass, and then appeared again, standing at the edge of the cemetery nearest to the canal. When the figure looked back through the leaning gravestones and long grass, and saw Mary standing by Albert's grave, it almost dropped the pink flask it was carrying. The figure grabbed wallflowers from the vase that sat on the grave nearest to it, and changed the water in the vase, using a tap nearby, all the time watching Mary, who was talking to Albert about what she would need to bring from the flat in order to set up house in the tomb of Adrian Stanley Winstanton. When the figure had replaced the wallflowers, it made its way slowly towards Mary, taking a roundabout route in order to catch her off guard. Mary saw the pink figure moving from gravestone to tomb, from tomb to weeping angel, getting closer and closer, and decided that it was time she went on her errand.

'I've got to go now, but I won't be long,' she said, looking in the direction of the pink figure. 'Don't go talking to any strangers, will you? Be back soon.'

The figure came from behind a large urn to reveal itself. Mary turned, flask in hand, and left the cemetery.

Mary returned to the cemetery an hour later, loaded down with what she needed for her new home. First she had gone back to the flat, and got two blankets and some warm clothes. There was nothing in the cupboard to eat, except two tins of baked beans and half a stale loaf. Mary packed them into a large suitcase with the blankets, and went out shopping.

Mary bought:

> 4 pkts Custard Creams
> ¾ lb tea (Green Label)
> 4 lbs sugar
> 2 tins powdered milk
> 2 large sliced loaves
> ½ lb butter
> ½ lb bacon
> ½ lb beef sausages
> 4 tins tomatoes (small)
> 4 med size Heinz Beef Broth
> 1 primus stove and 1 bottle methylated spirits
> 1 bottle Jeyes' Pine Disinfectant
> 2 doz candles

When she got back to the flat, she added a frying pan, a

kettle, a tin-opener, a scrubbing brush and a knife, fork and spoon to the other items in the suitcase.

Four carrier bags and a suitcase were as much as Mary could carry, and when the pink figure (which was just about to leave the cemetery) saw her staggering through the gates, loaded down with them, it offered to lend a hand.

The woman's fingers were toying with the locks of the suitcase. 'I just popped round the corner to get his suits dry-cleaned,' Mary said, and moved the suitcase out of reach. They sat together on the Chinaman's grave, and the woman poured them tea from her new pink flask.

At ten to six, the woman got up to leave, and Mary pretended to add up her shopping, and try to find the apricot jam she was sure she had bought. When the woman was out of sight, Mary dragged the suitcase to the tea importer's tomb, and then came back for the carrier bags. She was sure that, if she waited until 7 p.m. before frying herself supper, no one would be bothered by the smell.

Unknown to Mary, the woman in pink had waited outside the gates for her. At six thirty, when the gates had been locked for half an hour and the woman's thin legs were beginning to tire and it seemed clear that Mary intended to stay the night, the woman tightened her grip round the shiny pink flask, and mounted a Number 43 homeward, her suspicions confirmed.

When Mary rose again on the third day, it was going to be a difficult one.

She had lived happily for two days, talking with Albert until it had got dark, then sitting by candlelight in the tomb of the tea importer until she fell asleep. Since she intended to live there indefinitely, she had scrubbed out the floor with disinfectant and water, which was available at various parts of the cemetery. Mary thought that, if Albert ever did manage to get in touch with Adrian Stanley Winstanton (or, as

Albert had renamed him, 'Stan, Stan, the Dustbin Lid Man' –
the dustbin lid had been scrubbed too, and hung on one of
the walls), Mr Winstanton might feel happier about sharing
his tomb with Mary if she took on the job of unpaid house-
keeper, and did for him.

'I didn't see you leave last night.'

Mary had had a good night. Her sleep had been sound. The
tomb had smelt sweetly of Jeyes' Pine, and she had talked to
Albert for a long time until her jaw ached. Her meal had
been a little spoiled by her not being used to the ways of
Primus stoves, and by her having burnt three fingers and lost
the best part of an eyebrow. But cold baked beans are always
tasty, and she had finally managed to heat enough water for
tea. The tea was the best Mary had ever tasted.

'I hope you didn't get yourself locked in.'

She had lain in her blankets – blankets Albert had been
warmed by – and thought of subjects for conversation. Topics
that they could discuss at length. For now he never seemed
tired of talking, as he had in his living days. Then, they would
get to a certain point in an argument, usually when Mary
was winning, and he would say, 'Have you ever listened to
yourself, girl? You could talk the hind legs off a disc jockey.'
Now he seemed to enjoy long talks, even on subjects she had
never heard him speak of. And now if it came to an argument,
Mary found that she was only too happy to see that he won
with dignity.

'I know you couldn't have got over that wall, because I
tried it once, when I thought I was locked in.'

The woman in pink stood over Mary, while Mary pretended to be praying. 'How rude,' thought Mary, 'to talk to
someone, when the someone is supposed to be having a conversation with God.' She had seen the pink figure running
through the gates (rude to run in a cemetery) the moment the
little man had pushed them open.

'I'd be scared out of my wits, if I had to stay in here all night.'

Mary's knees were beginning to hurt. She had adopted this position, hands clasped, elbows resting on Albert's mound, when she had seen the pink figure darting in and out between the graves, making a bee-line towards her. When the woman arrived, breathless, and croaked, 'Where were you, then?' Mary had countered with a loud 'Give us this day our daily bread.' She then had to finish the prayer, which she was not altogether sure of, so she quickly changed to a passionate sibilant whisper, naming the days of the week and the months of the year in a voice that was too quiet to be heard. It was giving her time to think of a reply, though thinking was not made easy by the woman leaning over her, gasping such breaths and sighing such sighs.

'It'd be like one of those horror films, where they give you a prize if you're a woman and can sit it through without screaming or being sick.'

Mary mouthed all the girls' names she could think of, and hoped that the woman might see someone else she knew. One of the gardeners perhaps.

'Here! Are you Catholic?'

'No, why?'

'You've been down there nearly half an hour. God, I was scared when I thought I was locked in. You should have heard me rattle that gate until a policeman came, and went for the key. You didn't stay in here all night, did you?'

There was nothing for it but to tell the truth. The woman was clearly not going to be put off, and if Mary were rude, she would surely cause trouble.

'Yes, and the night before.'

'Haven't you got a home, then?'

'Come and see.' The full story had to be told. She was not the sort of woman to make do with half.

Mary crept through the bottom part of Mr Winstanton's door, and the woman reluctantly followed, mumbling about there being rats or skeletons, and perhaps both. Mary lit the candle, and the woman surveyed the room.

'What's the dustbin lid for?'

'Decoration.' The woman had no imagination. 'It was here already.'

There were lots of questions, and the woman asked them all. It was not until she had exhausted the practical difficulties of living there, that she came to the reason for it.

They crept stealthily out into the daylight in order to save candles. When the woman heard of Albert and his conversations with Mary, her face sagged, and Mary thought she was going to cry.

'I went to a spiritualist once, but Mother refused to communicate. No one could have done more than I have. Yours is all right; he's in the dry. All we need is a couple of weeks' rain, and she'll be swimming in it. I think it was 1959 it rained for ten days solid. I had to cover her up with plastic raincoats.' At this point, the woman in pink did break down and grab Mary's hand with her claw-like fingers.

Mary stood in the middle of Kensal Green Cemetery, holding hands with a woman she hardly knew, and watching her tight bony face screw itself up with each spasm of sorrow. Her tears, which Mary imagined to be very salty, poured out of eye-sockets that were vermilion.

'I always told her that if I ever won the Pools, I'd have her moved into something special up at the posh part.' The woman loosened her grip on Mary's hand, and Mary knew that she would be unable to lift anything with it for some time. The tears were now a mere trickle, and the woman had settled for occasional sobs, which jarred her shoulders. 'Have you seen this?' she said. 'That's how I'd have her done.'

They were standing before the tomb of Major General Sir

William Casement, K.C.B., of the Bengal Army, a member of the Supreme Council of the Government of India. Mounted on an enormous dais stood a stone coffin, guarded at each corner by four figures. Lying on top of the coffin were a stone cloak, a stone sword, and two larger-than-life stone hats, one formal, one casual. The heads of the figures held the three-feet-thick concrete canopy in place; their arms were crossed across their chests. Around the base of the tomb, ten rusted iron bollards supported a spiked chain, each link the size of a hand. The long inscription was unreadable, save for the last three words, 'HIS PRIVATE WORTH'. 'He won't get damp up there,' the woman said.

They moved back to Albert's grave, and Mary was asked questions. Questions about almost everything. The woman had an insatiable hunger for every detail of Mary's life, particularly the details concerning her marriage and her parents.

When the woman left, protesting that she would tell no one of Mary's new home, Mary felt drained and depressed. She had given away intimate details of her life with Albert. She had spoken of private references and jokes that they had shared, and the woman had constantly asked for more.

For the next few days, the woman arrived early and stayed late, always bringing small gifts of cake or chocolate, and always sitting beside Mary on the Chinaman's grave, asking questions. Eventually Mary ran out of answers, and started to invent. Every now and then, the woman begged Mary to talk to Albert, and let her listen. Mary explained that Albert's voice was inside her head, and although she repeated aloud what he said, it was she who was speaking, and no one could hear Albert but herself.

'I would like to explain to Mother about the dampness of her grave.' The woman placed the pink flask on the Chinaman's marble, her eyes brimming with tears again. 'Ask Albert if he's met her.'

Mary was tired.

'You never know; they might be good friends, like we are. Her married name was Florence Henderson, but she may have gone back to her maiden, which was Lindley. You ask him.'

Mary said she would ask him later that night, when he would be in a good mood. The woman's face tightened.

'You don't want to ask him, do you? You're afraid of what he'll say. You're afraid he'll say she won't talk to me, aren't you?'

Mary explained that this was not the case.

'You said you could talk to him at any time. Ask him now. If she says, No, this time, I won't ask her again.' The woman had unwrapped some sliced bread, and was throwing bits of the crust to three sparrows. 'It's not much of a favour to ask, is it?'

Mary's hatred of the woman frightened her. Closing her eyes, she laid one hand on Albert's black marble vase. The woman was impressed, and Mary, squinting slightly through her eyelashes, noticed it.

'Albert!'

The woman leaned forward, and supported herself, one hand resting on Albert's mound, somewhere in the region of his private parts. Mary removed the woman's spiky fingers, and motioned her to sit still.

'Albert! Albert, are you free to talk?' The game was so silly that Mary almost laughed out loud. 'Albert, can you hear?' There was no answer. She had expected him to say something rude. 'Albert, it's Mary. I have an inquiry here from a lady whose name I don't know.'

'Angela.'

Mary saw Albert's face clearly. His forefinger pressed his nose upwards to resemble a pig, and his thumb dragged his lower lip to one side, allowing his bottom false teeth to jut out. That was Albert's imitation of the Beast in a horror film they had seen together. The Beast was a man who had injected himself with the hormones of a pig: the film didn't explain why. Albert pulled this face whenever they had pork for lunch.

'I don't think he's there.'

'Try again.'

'Albert, we're trying to get in touch with a Mrs Henderson.'

'Or Lindley.'

'Or Lindley.'

'She died in 1955.'

'She's been there some time, Albert.' Mary's voice trembled with control. Albert was gesturing and making faces, but refusing to speak.

When Mary did speak to Albert later that evening, she spoke of her fear. Once it was clear that she was not going to hear Albert's voice, or receive a message from her mother, the woman had become calm. Calm in a way that frightened Mary. There were no more tears. Her voice was quiet, as she stood on her thin legs to tidy her clothes. Mary had said that she would keep trying, but the woman seemed to have lost interest, and left, telling her not to bother.

Albert must invent messages from the woman's mother, and Mary would pass them on. It was the only thing to do. Mary tried to remember all she had been told about 'Mother'. It was not a great deal.

It was lunch-time before the pink figure walked slowly through the gates. There was no flask in her hand, and she was not coming towards Mary; she was going towards the graves nearest the canal. Mary ran between the gravestones, shouting, 'I've got a message for you.' The woman stopped, but her head remained lowered. Mary told her how Albert had come across this old lady in a large hat, pruning roses with

31

silver secateurs. And how the old lady had told him that her name was Henderson, late Lindley, and that she had a daughter, but was not in the least damp. She wished to send her love to her daughter, Angela, and would have done so in person, but had only recently found out that this was possible. Nice as it was there, they were, she said, a little disorganized. However, she had now applied for permission to talk to her daughter direct and was waiting for her case to be heard.

Mary gave the woman this explanation bit by bit, as Albert had given it to her. The woman inquired what had happened to her mother's hay-fever, that she was now able to work in the garden so happily. Mary, who was stumped, said that it did seem odd, but while they were pouring fresh water into the old woman's flowers, Albert came up with the answer. Hay-fever was to do with pollen, and pollen was to do with reproduction, but since nothing where Albert and Mother were ever died, there was no cause for pollen. Mary then promised to ask Albert about bees.

The woman looked much prettier when she smiled. She was clearly delighted. She remembered once having bought Mother a large straw hat when they had visited Lyme Regis. She had unstitched the ribbon which said, 'I GIVE GREEN STAMPS', and replaced it with a plain pink one. She giggled. She could not thank Mary enough. Mary grasped her opportunity, and said that she would do all she could, but that it was more likely that Albert would talk to her if she was on her own. The woman left, saying that she was sorry she had forgotten to bring any cake.

'A Miss Henderson came to see me, Mary. She was worried about your sanitary arrangements.'

He was rubbing his head, and crushing the tuft of grey hair which Mary had thought was a fairy.

'Are you all right?'

'Yes, of course,' he said, with some pain. 'I'm just not accustomed to using only the bottom half of a door. Is that your piece of modern art?' He had changed the subject by pointing to the dustbin lid. The vicar was a free-thinking liberal intellectual, who found life unbearable unless he was making a joke of it.

Mary removed her bacon from the primus stove, and made them tea. They talked for two hours. She had never in her life had such a lengthy conversation, and certainly never one so interesting.

'Let us start by admitting that there is wrong on both our sides.' His name was John, and he liked to be addressed by it.

'I, if you try to stay here, will be professionally embarrassed. You, on the other hand, are taking advantage of the dead.'

He was proud, he said, to have helped her to a way of life (using her memories, properly) that suited her, but was it not possible to combine it with another flat, which he himself would help her to find? Mary explained that a flat would cost money, and that she had no training for a job. Even if she had, it would take up too much time – time she wished to devote to Albert. If, as John said, Albert would follow her anywhere, she would look for another home, one less public. She had become fond of waking with the birds; it meant her day was longer, and therefore her time with Albert.

But if she stayed, Miss Henderson would continue to worry.

No, she did not miss a proper bed. 'Beds are for two people.' She had never wanted gadgets, and television made her sleepy.

When John left at about nine thirty, they had struck a bargain. John had promised that, if Albert refused to leave Kensal Green Cemetery and go with Mary, he would try to think of a place in which Mary could live rent-free, and visit Albert during open hours. This was not a difficult bargain for John, because he had an ace up his sleeve, though it was

33

an ace Mary might refuse to accept. The ace was National Assistance.

John sniffed the air, inhaling the smell of damp stone mingled with Jeyes' Pine. 'I envy you the open-air life. I once went hiking in the Cairngorms. It was on that beautiful holiday that I almost decided against the church. I wanted to be a comedian. But I should never have been as funny as Max Miller.'

# THE FACTS OF LIFE

*Money*

Albert's insurance policy paid Mary £1,000 *plus bonuses*.
The funeral and black marble vase had taken care of the
*bonuses* and a little more besides.

The man who delivered the cheque to her explained that
she must deposit it at a bank or a Post Office. Mary had an
old Post Office Savings Book, which still had one and nine-
pence in it, so she added the cheque to that. The Post Office
told her that they would give her interest at two and a half
per cent, but she didn't understand.

Albert's firm had sent her a letter saying that they were
unable to pay compensation, since Albert's fall could not be
classified as an industrial accident. Mary did careful sums, and
worked out that by drawing only one pound a week she could
manage on Albert's insurance money until she was sixty, and
entitled to the Old Age Pension.

John the Vicar's ace was not really an ace at all, for Mary
would not be granted National Assistance with £1,000 in the
Post Office.

*Food*

Before leaving the tomb of Adrian Stanley Winstanton,
Mary had a feast. She consumed:
Half a sliced loaf, with butter half an inch thick

5 rashers of bacon

4 sausages

2 small tins of tomatoes (heated)

1 medium sized tin of Heinz Beef Broth (ditto)

5 cups of Green Label Tea with four spoonfuls of sugar in each cup (for energy)

This was all food which she did not wish to carry with her.

From now on, economies would have to be made. Mary's daily ration would be:

1 apple or orange: 7d.

1 packet of Crisps: 6d. (Cheese-and-Onion or Plain, the Vinegar or Bacon ones being too salty)

1 carton of milk: 6d.

1 meat pie or sausage roll: 7d.

TOTAL: 2s 2d. (This was well within her budget)

She realized that now and then she would lose sixpence in a faulty milk machine, and this would have to be made up by economies elsewhere.

Without knowing it, Mary had picked a healthy diet for someone who is not working, and takes frequent rests. (Later, when she began walking all day, twelve to fifteen miles every day, it was far too little.)

Mary left the primus stove in the tomb with all the cooking utensils. She poured the remainder of the Jeyes' Pine Disinfectant around Albert's grave to discourage earwigs.

## Clothing

Replacing clothes would be expensive. Mary decided to wear as many of her clothes as she could, and carry what was left. This would include her wedding dress, which she would keep until all else had worn out.

Mary only had two pairs of shoes, and one pair hurt her, so that pair would be left behind.

## Rent

The rent of the flat was six pounds a week. It had to be paid a month in advance, and it was almost due when Mary went to live in the cemetery.

She had drawn £24 out of the Post Office, and left it in an envelope on the sideboard, with a note saying that she would not be coming back, and that she was sorry for the crack which had appeared in the wash-hand basin.

## Childhood

Mary had been a large girl, not fat but with big bones. Neither ugly nor pretty, she had worn her hair in ringlets up to the day of her wedding to Albert. Every night before she went to bed, she would kneel at her mother's feet and have her hair wrapped round and round in white cotton rags. It was the only time of day, except for meals and milking, her mother sat down. Running a farm is a busy life, more so for the wife than the husband.

Mary's mother had taken special care with the ringlets on Mary's wedding morning. Four long ones trailed over her shoulders, irritating the back of her neck, and three small dinky ones on either side of her ears bobbed up and down, just in her field of vision. Mary sneaked a hair-brush in among the carnations of her bouquet, and brushed them all out in the car on the way to church. It was a windy day, and the heavily brushed hair blew across and covered her face on all the photographs. Mary's mother cried, and left the reception early to help with the evening milking.

## Sex: Female

She had seen the local boar serving one of her father's sows.

It was his third serving that day, so he had to be helped up into position. She remembered the shaking and wobbling of his flesh and the sow's, as he jerked his back parts. After three or four of these jerks, the sow had given a scream, and run away, leaving the puzzled boar with his front legs in the air and his pink stair-rod sticking out in front of him. The two farmers had retired to the nearest pub, and then returned an hour later to try again. The sow was coaxed back close to the boar, and he was lifted on again. This time, the man who had brought him played with the boar's private parts, to arrange the necessary part into a good position for the sow. The sow lifted her head, and gave long low grunts. Mary could not tell if this were pain or pleasure, but since the sow remained where she was with the boar on her back, it seemed all right.

Coming home from school one day, she was just in time to see a cow licking the blood off its newly born calf. The mother walked meticulously round her baby, licking every inch of it, and trailing her long scarlet umbilical cord behind her. The sight of this shiny red rope, dangling out of the cow's rear, prevented Mary from putting tomato ketchup on her food for several weeks.

*Children: None*

Because Mary had seen these things, her parents thought it unnecessary to talk to her about the facts of life. So that when Mary married Albert, she had only a basic knowledge of sexual intercourse, and knew none of its finer points. Albert, however, knew all these points, and quickly enlightened her. He gave her what he described as a Nature Study Lesson.

Mary was told that, if they were not careful, Albert would spill himself inside her, planting his seed there, and that it would germinate, causing her to become pregnant (as the cow had been), and give birth (painful and some times dangerous) to a little one. Albert and she had decided that a little one was out of the question, until they had at least a hundred pounds in the bank. And somehow they never got anywhere near this figure.

In order to prevent a little one, Mary was to lie there and enjoy it (within reason), but not under any circumstances to hold, or pull, or wrap legs round, or jerk, or move at all in fact, once Albert had said, 'Stop!' and was practising his iron control. Albert's iron control was to withdraw himself quickly, spilling his seed safely on Mary's stomach. Mary always enjoyed sex with Albert, because the long stimulation which Albert performed before placing himself inside her never failed to give her a climax before his.

# A LUXURY FLAT

She had walked all day. Down the Harrow Road to Paddington, then down the Bayswater Road to Notting Hill. She had avoided Hyde Park, because it was a sunny day, and she knew that if once she sat down on the grass to rest and talk to Albert she would not have the strength of will to start walking again. It would be no good trying to spend the night in Hyde Park. Police prowled it, looking for courting couples.

From Notting Hill, she walked to Earls Court. She could not go back to the flat, even if she had wanted to, and she didn't. Someone else would be living there now. Would they, she wondered, be sleeping in the same bed? Perhaps they would be a young couple, newly married. The husband would have to fit into Albert's hollow, since the landlord was unlikely to have changed the mattress.

From Earls Court, she walked to Gloucester Road, and from Gloucester Road to South Kensington. Up to then, she had not known what she was looking for. Suddenly it was clear.

LUXURY FLATS

WITH SHOPS AND PARKING AREA

TO BE BUILT ON THIS SITE

BY J & B CONTRACTORS

Mary stood before a fence some nine feet high, the top of which had been fortified with barbed wire. A sign said that Trespassers would be Prosecuted, and the gates had been bolted from the inside.

While Mary walked round the corner and down an alley at the side of the site, she tried to work out how it was possible to lock something from the inside without locking oneself in as well. A small moth-eaten dog raised a leg to relieve itself against the fence. Unfortunately, the dog had chosen an insecure plank on which to place some of its weight. As the plank moved, the dog lost its balance, and also its urge to pee. With a look round at Mary, and a sniff, it moved on up the alley.

Mary bent down, and pressed the loose plank in order to see through the fence. Clearly the barbed wire and locks had been placed there in order to save J & B Contractors the expense of a night watchman, for the site was deserted.

After standing where she was, looking from right to left, Mary kicked the plank next to the loose one. Three kicks and it was free. Then she stood absolutely still for three minutes (a minute for each kick) in case anyone had heard.

When she had crept through the two loose planks, she closed them again behind her. The only windows overlooking the site were those belonging to offices, and it was now after office hours.

Small ditches had been dug like graves, and large drainpipes stood by them, waiting to be buried. There were no trees, and no flowers or long grass. But if Mary half-closed her eyes, each pile of window-frames, each concrete mixer, each stack of timber or scaffolding could look like a tomb. Certainly the enormous earth-digger, with its fork-pronged shovel, small chimney and large pistons, reminded her of the tomb of Major General the Right Honourable Sir William Casement, K.C.B., of the Bengal Army, and that was without closing her eyes.

'You could go farther and find worse,' Albert said. Which was what he had said when they found the flat in Willesden.

Mary climbed the stairs of the unfinished skyscraper. On the third floor, she spread out her blankets, and lay down on top of them to think about sleep. She would wake with the sunlight, and be gone before anyone started work.

Nobody would come visiting here. Not out of working hours.

# MILDLY SUBNORMAL

Mary was happy. She had been living in her unfurnished luxury flat for two weeks now. And she could talk to Albert whenever she felt like it.

Her day would be spent walking about. She never walked too far or too fast, and there were always parks in which to rest.

The hour which she enjoyed most out of the twenty-four was the one before sleep, when she would lie, looking at the concrete ceiling, stroking the blankets beside her, and talking with Albert. This made her very happy.

When the Sales were in full swing, Mary took Albert down to Oxford Street. C and A was their favourite shop. The heat rushed at you as you opened the door, and the sudden change of temperature made you gasp.

Mary liked this shop best because she could stand in it, watching all sorts of women trying on all sorts of dresses and suits. They would disappear into the little cubicles, carrying the dresses of their choice – they were only allowed three at a time – and they would reappear transformed. Mary would nod if she liked the transformation, or shake her head if she disapproved. Sometimes she shook her head violently even before the woman had got inside the cubicle, but this usually meant that she didn't like the look of the woman, and had no bearing on the dress.

Albert was always very talkative on these occasions. He

had a keen eye for what Mary should wear, and voiced his opinion. Blue was too common, and red was gaudy. Pink was pretty, but a little childish. Green was a favourite, but best of all was white. White always did; you could never be caught out with white.

They would decide on white, and pick out something Mary herself would have bought if she could have afforded it. She never minded not having the money to spend, for, as Albert always said, 'Never buy on impulse. There's always tomorrow.'

'Never buy on impulse,' Mary would repeat to a fat lady holding up a heavily flowered frock. 'There's always tomorrow.' Then Albert and Mary would stand in the doorway for a moment, warming themselves in the gush of heat before stepping out into the cold.

The egg-shaped hole in the sole of Mary's right shoe was now so large that it made the front half of the shoe flap ahead. Feeling the cool wet pavement underfoot was quite pleasant, but the monotonous flapping sound irritated her. And once she had stepped into some dog-shit. It was still warm. The slimy texture made her shiver, and the smell made her feel sick, so she threw away her left shoe.

In a square in Knightsbridge, she found a small concrete trough, on which was written 'LET YOUR DOGGY DRINK'. Mary washed her foot in it thoroughly. After all, it was only justice.

For two days she limped along wearing one shoe, sometimes on the foot it was made for (the right), and sometimes on the left so as not to develop a permanent limp. Because the shoe had been made for the right foot, when worn on the left it pushed the big toe towards the smaller ones, so that they huddled together, one on top of the other, like puppies in a basket. The pain was acute, and Mary could only put up with it for an hour at a time, but while putting up with it she

44

managed at the same time to enjoy it, for it seemed to help to cleanse the foot of dog-shit.

After two days of limping, Mary stepped into something else. It happened while she was giving her left foot its hourly purge, so this time the right suffered. It was in the gutter hidden by leaves, and she had stepped off the pavement to cross the Fulham Road.

'It could have happened to anybody. You sit still now. You going to be as right as April showers.'

'I should have seen it.'

'No use crying over spilt milk bottles, is there?' He pressed a shining black thumb on the vein, and held the bleeding foot away from the whiter-than-white coat. 'You certainly know where to have your accidents. We just round the corner from St Stephen's.'

Mary's blood had made a large dark pool on the pavement.

'How them folks in Onslow Square going to walk their dogs on that bloody pavement?'

Mary laughed.

They had given her a local anaesthetic, and taken three pieces of broken milk bottle out of her foot. Mary sat waiting for an ambulance to come and take her to an address which didn't exist. On admittance, they had asked for her name and address. The address she had given was one made up on the spur of the moment, '12, Albert Square, Willesden.' After the operation, they had sat her in a wheelchair, and told her not to stand or walk on the foot for at least three days. She had then been wheeled out into Reception, and told that an ambulance would take her home.

'I'm not going back to the old flat. They'll have let it by now.' Mary was speaking to herself as much as to Albert, but Albert answered just the same.

'Well, you can't walk around on that foot. And you can't

sit here for three days. They'll need the wheelchair, for one thing.'

Mary's habit of not only talking to Albert out loud, but also voicing his thoughts for him in a voice that mimicked his, worried the other patients waiting to be healed.

'What are you going to do when they find out there's no Albert Square in Willesden, and even if there is, you don't belong in it?' A chain-smoking woman in a headscarf sought the attention of a nurse, and told her to listen to the woman in the wheelchair. Mary was totally unaware that she was being observed.

'You know I can't go back to Park Street.'

'Well, you'd better think of somewhere you can sit down for three days, and then ask the ambulance men to take you there. That building site won't do. There'll be workmen all over the place.'

'Are you worried about getting home? Try not to. The ambulance will be here soon. Is anyone waiting for you?' The cheerful healthy nurse squatted down in order to catch Mary's eye.

'No. I'm sorry, I told the other nurse a lie. There is no Albert Square in Willesden. Albert was my husband. He's not there any more, so I can't go back. They must have re-let it by now. I left them a note about the crack in the basin. It wasn't the same without Albert. Will you ask the ambulance men to drop me off at Kensal Green Cemetery? I know where I can sit down for three days, and it won't be out of their way.'

The nurse left, saying she would come back. Mary watched her go behind the Reception Desk, and talk to the women there, who had stopped work to look at her.

Suddenly Mary's wheelchair began to move. 'You're for Albert Square, aren't you, love?'

'No!' Mary grabbed the wheels to stop the chair, and trapped her finger badly. After letting out a scream, she began to sob with pain and frustration.

'It's all right, Bill; you'd better leave this one. She doesn't live in Willesden.'

'But it says so here.'

'We were misinformed. What's wrong with her?'

'She grabbed hold of the spokes. I couldn't stop her. I think it's more shock than anything else, sister.'

'All right. I'll deal with it.'

Sister was to deal with it, so Mary was wheeled into her office, sobbing.

'Have you any family, Mary?' Sister sat at her desk, and switched on the table lamp, so as to be able to make notes. Since the lie about Albert Square had caused so much trouble, it was clearly best to tell the truth. Mary explained to Sister about the building site. A doctor was sent for. The doctor asked more questions.

'What day is it today, Mary?'

Mary had no idea. One day was like another to her. If you're walking about, it makes no difference. Except for Sundays. One can always tell it's Sunday by the number of people about. Fewer.

'It's not a Sunday.'

'No, it's not a Sunday.'

There was too much traffic for a Sunday; she always knew when it was Sunday. If it wasn't Sunday, then it made no difference to Mary what day it was. But this was not what the doctor and the sister wished to hear. To them it obviously mattered a great deal what name the day had.

They were watching her, waiting for her to say something. It was like school. You'd been caught not listening. Now you were asked a question, and you had to say something and run the risk of being laughed at.

'It feels as if it could be Wednesday.'

Wednesday was the middle of the week, so there seemed

more chance of its being Wednesday. The doctor and Sister exchanged a look, and Mary knew she had failed. Why was it so important?

Sister took from her pocket a man's handkerchief with a blue border, and blew her nose heartily. The border matched her uniform.

'What would you have done, Mary, if the ambulance men had taken you to Kensal Green Cemetery, as you asked?'

The doctor hadn't known this, so they exchanged another meaningful glance, while Sister replaced the handkerchief, and smoothed the front of her uniform.

'There's a tomb. It belongs to a tea importer, Mr Winstanton. I've left a primus stove, a dustbin lid, and one or two other things in it. I could sit there.'

'For three days?'

'The vicar said I could always come back if it was really necessary. He wouldn't mind. His name's John.'

'What's the name of the Prime Minister, Mary?'

They were making fun of her. They were laughing at her without smiling. Asking silly questions. They weren't trying to understand; they didn't want to. Mary's stomach began to make noises. It always did when she was nervous. Also she hadn't eaten all day.

'I don't know what you mean. What's he got to do with Kensal Green Cemetery?'

'Nothing at all. I just wondered if you knew his name.'

Mary's stomach made a louder noise.

'I beg your pardon. It's my stomach. It's upset.'

'Sister will get you something to eat, won't you, Sister?' Sister left the room.

'Now, if I'm counting backwards from ten, what comes after four?'

'Five.'

'No, I'm counting backwards.'

'Why? Are you making fun of me? Hospitals are supposed to cure you, not ask silly questions, and make you feel nervous. I don't appreciate that.' She was very close to tears now, and wanted to talk to Albert. 'If dogs weren't allowed to dirty the pavement, I wouldn't be here to be laughed at.'

'I'm not laughing at you, Mary. I'm trying to help you, really I am. Here's Sister, with something for you to eat. I think Mary should stay in hospital for a few days, Sister. Certainly until her foot is better, and there's no risk of infection. I'll ring round, and see where we can fit her in.'

Mary pulled herself away from sleep, and smelt the combined smell of herself and carbolic. It reminded her of the evenings when, so as not to offend him, she had washed and rinsed herself twice all over before getting into bed with Albert.

'You always smell of soap, girl.'

The white shroudlike nightie had been starched so much that it stood away from her like a tube filled with warm air. Lifting the lower half of her body, she touched it with her belly and thighs. Its smooth stiffness fascinated her. She rubbed her pubic hair against it gently. Since she had got used to wearing the same heavy layers of clothing, this was almost a new experience. The small cupboard beside her bed contained nothing but a bottle of water and a glass. It was clearly too small to hold her coat and dresses, her one shoe and her bundle. Mary supposed that they must have been locked away in Sister's office.

The ward was a large one, containing some twenty beds or more. It was noisy. Two people were crying. Mary wondered why no one asked the reason. One patient was teaching another to say in Pakistani that she had piles. Another shouted 'Nurse! Nurse! Frizzy black bitch!' at irregular intervals. In the next bed to Mary, a woman sat bolt upright, staring ahead of her. Below her eyes were large red circles, and her fingers plucked continuously at the bedclothes. An old lady in a very dirty dressing-gown walked up and down between the beds, singing to the other patients. At each bed she would start a new song, and, even if discouraged by the occupant, would insist on finishing it before moving on to the next.

Visiting Hour arrived, and Mary watched four visitors walk into the ward. Of the twenty patients, only three had visitors. Two had come to see an old lady who kept crying.

Discovering earphones beside the bed, Mary put them on, and was told the News. None of it had anything to do with her, and the Racing Results seemed to go on forever, so she changed channels, found Mantovani, and wondered what the B.B.C. would do without him.

Next day, Mr Smith came to see her. He was a small man with ginger freckles, and two strands of very blond hair.

'Good morning. You're Mary.'

'Yes.'

He sat in the chair beside her bed, and arranged the pens in his top pocket. There were several. There was also a silver propelling pencil.

'How's the foot?'

'I think it's all right.'

'Good.'

Having arranged the pens, he plucked them all out of his pocket again with a click, click, click, and studied them.

'I just want to ask you some questions.'

'What about?'

He chose the red one, and flicked it towards the floor, testing it for ink-content.

'About you.'

He was ready now. As though the key had been turned, and the safe unlocked, he went to work, stealing the valuables.

'What's your full name, Mary?'

'Mary Watson.'

'Just Mary? Not Mary Jane? Or Mary Poppins?' He laughed.

'Just Mary.'

'When were you born?'

'I'm forty-six.'

'What year is that?'

Before agreeing to go into hospital, Mary had insisted that no screens should be placed round her bed, because she knew that this was what hospital people did when you were about to die; if she was going to die, she didn't want to know about it until she was dead. Consequently, Mr Smith had decided to attempt this interview without them, and to use as little voice as possible in order to create a feeling of privacy. Mary found it difficult to catch all of what he said. And from time to time, the other patients would try to attract his attention.

'How can they expect you to get well, when the lavatory doors have no locks?' The woman in the next bed was returning from the bathroom.

Mary could not remember the year of her birth, but she knew she was forty-six.

'We'll leave that one. Are you married?'

'Yes.'

'What about children?'

'The twenty-first of September, 1923; that's my birthday. I've just worked it out. I'm a Virgo, you see.'

'Give her a bath, nurse, for God's sake. She comes slinking round my bed, stinking of last month's curse, and offering me toffees!'

'You filthy-minded slut!'

'Slinking and stinking! Stinking and slinking!'

A nurse attempted to part the two women, who were biting and scratching each other.

'Did you ever have any children, Mary?'

'Once they get you in here, you know, they sterilize you,

so you can't have any daft children.' This was the view of the lady in the dirty dressing-gown, who usually sang. She seated herself at the foot of Mary's bed, in order to take part in the interview.

'That will do, Adeline. Go away now. I'm busy. I'll get Nurse to find you a boiled sweet.' Clicking the red pen into his breast pocket, he stood up.

'He's very nice, isn't he? Do you fancy him?'

'No.'

'I do. It's the freckles. I've always liked them.' The old lady arranged the dirty dressing-gown around her, and settled comfortably on Mary's bed.

'Nurse!'

'How did they find you?'

'I cut my foot.'

'Did you? I put my head out of the door one morning, thinking it was the postman, and they grabbed me. The woman next door stood laughing. She said, "I told you they'd put you away some day."'

'Nurse, will you find Adeline a green boiled sweet? But only if she stays in bed, and can make it last for at least ten minutes.'

Adeline left, hand in hand with the large West Indian nurse, and Mr Smith sat down again.

'Now, where were we? Children. Shall I write down that you haven't got any?'

'Yes.'

'What's your husband's name?'

'Albert.'

'Where is he?'

Mary, without thinking, touched her head. 'Here.'

She knew at once she had done wrong. The little pink face with ginger freckles rose slowly from the neatly oblique handwriting, and twitched with interest. A large pink hand, too large for a small man, lifted itself above the pink skull, and rearranged the two strands of hair.

'I mean, he's dead, but ...'

'But what?'

'Well, I think about him a lot. And he comes back sometimes.'

'And you talk to him?'

'Yes.'

'You must have been very close.'

'We were. What I mean is, he doesn't really come back. I imagine he comes back, and I talk to him. I know he's not there really.'

'You just imagine.'

'Yes. It's as though he is there sometimes.'

'Does he ever tell you where he's come from?'

'No, I never ask him where he's been.'

'Were your parents about the same age?'

'Dad was sixty-two, and Mother was sixty-four.'

'I see.'

'When they died.'

'I don't suppose either of them had syphilis.'

'I don't think so. They would have said.'

He had filled the whole of a very large page with very small writing. A cup of tea and some pills were brought to the woman in the next bed. Nobody else was served with tea. Obviously the tea was to wash down the pills. The woman struck out at the tea, and hit the nurse just below the elbow. The cup and some of the tea landed on Mary's bed. The woman gripped the nurse's arm with both hands, and said, 'If it will help, they can take my head off, and put it on again.' Mr Smith removed the cup from Mary's counterpane.

'Were there any Fits, Alcoholism or Paralysis in your family?'

'No,' seemed to be the safe reply.

'Did any of your family try to commit suicide?'

'No.'

'Are you all right? I don't want to tire you.'

'Yes.'

'This is quite important if we're to get to the bottom of your problem.'

'You mean my foot?'

'Yes, well, that too.'

The woman in the next bed was held by one nurse, while another fed her the pills, dissolved in tea, from a cup with a spout.

'So there was no eccentricity at all in your family?'

'Do you mean, were they mad?'

'Not exactly mad. More odd.'

'No, but they sometimes said I was.' She laughed nervously, then stopped, but to her relief, he was laughing too.

'Well, we're all a little odd, don't you think?'

He put down the pad, clicked the red pen into its rightful place beside the green one, and moved forward a little in his chair. 'You've been walking about, haven't you?'

'Yes.' Mary liked him, and he seemed to like her. He had laughed at her joke.

'What's it like?'

Now the valuables had to be valued.

'It's interesting. You can see a lot.' In a moment, he would ask her where she slept.

'Do you talk to lots of people?'

'Not very much. They don't want to.' Mary knew that always when she lied, a red blotch would appear on the right side of her nose. Yet she would have to lie, or she would be asked to leave her luxury flat, as she had been asked to leave the cemetery.

'But you have Albert to talk to. How long have you been ... walking?'

'Since Albert went.'

'When was that?'

Mary began to dislike herself. The warmth of the nice soft bed, and the kind man talking to her and taking the trouble to write down so neatly all she said, made her feel sorry for herself. They had given her apple crumble for lunch, and that had reminded her of the Park Street flat and her kitchen. It was unfair.

Mr Smith's blue eyes were waiting. They moved from side to side, searching her face. He spoke in a whisper, confiding to her that it would give him pleasure to know.

'Mary, when did Albert go?'

'It's not fair.'

'I know. Was it long ago?'

'September the twenty-fourth. Three days after my birthday.'

'The last one?'

The tears were there. She couldn't help them.

'We'll talk again soon. Oh, by the way, the nurse removed these from your clothes.' He placed some of Mary's belongings on the bedside cabinet – a bit of string, a pencil, two pennies and a sixpence, her Post Office Savings Book.

'Where are my clothes?'

'I think they've been burned. They were very dirty, Mary. They'll give you nice clean ones when you leave.'

# KEEPING THE GRASS DOWN

The building was grey, and had a tower.

'It's a lot prettier inside, you know,' said Nurse Jean. Mary held tight to the nurse's hand.

'The walls are pale blue. And some are pink.' They had ridden on a bus from the centre of London, and Mary was feeling slightly sick.

'Do you like colours, Mary?' Mary's stomach grumbled. She was nervous.

'You don't have to stay here, you know. We don't want you to be unhappy. I hope you believe that.'

They walked between trees on a lawn which had recently been cut. Every few yards, there was a wooden bench for the comfort of the patients.

At one point, they passed a man who talked aloud to a friend at his side. The friend was called Sid. The only trouble was that Sid didn't exist. Mary realized that talking to Albert here would be difficult. She must be careful, otherwise they would think her mad.

'You're in that nice new building over there.' Nurse Jean pointed across a beautiful flower bed. 'I think all the nicest girls live there.'

She had thrown flowers. Destroyed them. Vases as well. She had thrown two vases of dahlias from one end of the ward to the other. One vase had hit a nurse, and the other had smashed against the wall. Scattering wet flowers on the floor; it had frightened her. She had never had a temper, and was unused to screaming. When she had explained why she

56

had done it, they had brought back all her clothes, which had not been burned after all. Every one had been washed, and ironed, and folded neatly. They had not washed her wedding dress, for fear of spoiling it. She had felt so ashamed that when they had asked her if she would like to go and live in the country for a while, when her foot was better, she had nodded. It was not to be for long. They simply wished to keep an eye on her, and build her up a little.

'We'll be in time for lunch. I'll stay and have it with you, if you like.'

The lounge seemed to be full of chairs. In some of them, women sat, wearing dressing-gowns. Two were having their hair curled, and one was reading a book. A young girl, who knelt with her head on an older woman's lap, smiled and said 'Hello' as Mary entered. Mary continued to look round the room. She counted three women who just sat staring at the wall, and another who was trying to smoke a piece of rolled-up toilet paper.

'It's all right; she's trying to give up smoking. Come and sit here.' The young girl patted the seat next to the woman whom she was leaning against, and Mary sat.

'Do you want your hair done?' Mary shook her head. 'You'll have to get your name down, if you change your mind. Valerie does all our hair.'

'I wish I could change my mind. Anyone want to swap?' said a fat woman, who was having her hair done. Four of the others laughed.

Valerie twisted the fat woman's hair round blue plastic rollers. All the women's stockings hung round their ankles. None of them seemed to wear garters. But the walls were pale blue. And some of them were pink. It was quieter here than at the hospital. Much quieter.

\*  \*  \*

Each of them ate two gammon rashers with one pineapple ring, and after lunch Nurse Jean put an arm round Mary's shoulder, and whispered that she must catch the bus back. She explained that Mary must ask Sister Betty if there was anything she needed.

As Mary watched Nurse Jean walk across the recently cut lawn towards the gate, an old woman got up from one of the benches, and stopped her. Nurse Jean gave the old woman a cigarette from inside her blouse, and walked on. Nurse Jean was a Special Nurse, and had a medal to prove it.

Sister Betty showed Mary where she was to sleep, and told her that anyone with the name of Mary was eligible to become a close friend of hers. When Mary asked the young girl, Ruth, what this meant, Ruth said that it was because Sister Betty was Irish.

She was to share a room with two other women, one of them being Ruth. And it was Ruth and Mary who were to become close friends. The room was a pleasant one, with three beds, three cupboards, and three shelves for photographs. Mary had no photographs, and she placed her belongings under the bed, where they would be safe.

That evening Mary sat in the lounge, playing Newmarket for matches with Ruth and two other women. At nine o'clock, after supper, everyone moved into another room to watch the television, and Mary was shown which armchair to sit in. Ruth immediately knelt down beside her, and placed her head in Mary's lap. At first Mary was embarrassed by this, until she saw that several of the other women held hands, and behaved affectionately towards each other. The woman whom Mary had first seen nursing Ruth's head did not seem worried by Ruth's change in affection.

Mary was to spend the next few days 'settling down'. Since it was sunny and warm for October, and since her foot was almost completely healed, she was allowed to walk wherever she wished, providing that she was back in good time for meals.

Ruth walked Mary round and round the gardens to exercise Mary's foot. While they walked, they talked about the staff and the other patients. Ruth never questioned Mary about herself, and Mary never asked anything personal of Ruth. This, Mary thought, was the main reason they were becoming so close. She was happy not to be asked embarrassing questions about herself, but she would have liked to know what Ruth was suffering from.

At meal times, they walked back through one of the large corridors of the main building. There were four of these, each with five smaller corridors off it. All the large corridors seemed to be full of doors, and quite often a nurse would pass through one of these doors, locking it behind her. Mary wondered why there were so many store cupboards, and why they all needed locking.

The first time they had walked along one of the large corridors, Mary had stopped to watch an old man with a trolley clean up a mess from the floor. Ruth explained that one of the patients had not made it to the lavatory in time, and had relieved herself on the floor.

Further along the corridor, Mary stopped to look out through one of the windows. On a quadrangle of lawn, which the main building seemed to surround, four large lawn-mowers were being pulled and pushed by women patients. Each mower had two women at the front, pulling it by a rope, and two more held a handle each and pushed the mower from the rear. The four mowers moved backwards and forwards over the same blades of grass again and again, as though, if it were left for a moment, the grass would shoot up and become impossible to control. Mary was reminded of the dray horses she had once seen performing at an Agricultural Show.

Some of the women looked alike, their hair being cut short

and straight. Most of them wore skirts and cardigans, and all of them wore either ankle-socks or stockings which had been allowed to fall loosely around their ankles. These made their feet look like hooves. A person in a brown boiler-suit was raking a gravel path. At first Mary thought this person was a man, until she noticed the roundness of the person's breasts.

A very large woman in blue ankle socks and a pink hair-ribbon caught sight of Mary watching, and waved her hand, flapping it like a child's. Ruth took hold of Mary's arm and guided her away, saying that they would be late for lunch. She asked Mary not to worry about the women they had seen, because what they were doing was physiotherapy, and they were quite happy. She explained that drugs couldn't help them because they were too far gone. They would never get better, but since not getting better was all they knew, she considered that they couldn't be very unhappy about it. It was harder, she said, for anyone like herself, or Mary.

Mary did not understand why it should be harder for her, or indeed what should be harder, and as far as she could see there seemed to be nothing at all wrong with Ruth. Another thing she didn't understand was a word Ruth had used about the cart-horse women. The word was 'institutionalized'. When later she asked Ruth, who had been to Night School, what the word meant, Ruth said it meant that the cart-horse women would stay there for the rest of their lives. Mary realized why the lawn was so neat.

Albert had been silent for some time, except for a short while every night, when Mary placed her head underneath the bedclothes and whispered to him. But Mary didn't con-sider these real conversations. Occasionally, if she wanted the answer to a question quickly, she would go and sit on the lavatory and talk to him there, but only if she could be sure that there was nobody in any of the other cubicles.

Generally, Albert's view was that Mary was all right where

she was for the time being, specially since she was getting free meals and medical attention, but that she must certainly make it plain that she did not intend to stay and pull a mowing-machine around. He too liked Ruth, and thought that Mary was lucky to have her as a friend.

Mary had been 'settling down' now for a week and two days. The friendship between her and Ruth had grown stronger. They continued to take walks together, and sit together at meal times, and in the evening they would brush each other's hair before going down to sit in the lounge. Always they consulted each other on what they should do next.

Suddenly Ruth surprised Mary by asking who Albert was. Mary explained that he was dead. Ruth then took hold of Mary's hands, and asked her not to tell her any secrets, so Mary told her all about Albert. When she had finished, Ruth told Mary about her mother. It seemed that Ruth hated her mother.

The next day, Mary woke to find that Ruth and the other woman with whom she shared a room had gone down to breakfast without her. Washing quickly, she wondered why she had overslept, and why Ruth had not shaken her awake, as she had done every other morning.

Most of the women were still at breakfast, but Mary could find Ruth nowhere. When she asked the woman they called Fat Lady, she was told that Ruth was with Sister.

After breakfast, Mary went to sit in the lounge. She had no wish to start her walk without Ruth. When she had been sitting there for ten minutes, the door was flung open, and Ruth pointed at Mary, and screamed, 'There she is. Search her. Go on, search her. She's got my money.'

Mary's tongue swelled like a sponge. It seemed to be double its size, filling her mouth. And yet it was dry, and so was her mouth. Drained of all liquid, she gawped, looked at by everyone, watched by the women in the room.

Ruth clutched a tiny lace handkerchief in her right hand, while tears streamed down her face, and she shouted to anyone who might be near, begging them to search Mary and retrieve her two pounds.

'Mary's your friend, Ruth. Why should she steal from you?' Sister Betty held tight to both of Ruth's arms, as she guided her down into an armchair.

'Not my friend. Not my bloody friend.' Mary had never heard Ruth swear before. She wished to protest, but the dryness of her mouth would not allow it.

'Look at her. She looks guilty. Why doesn't she say something?' Mary stood, moving her lips, but no sound came out.

'She had the best opportunity. No wonder I've had underwear missing. Nothing's safe here. A friend!' Ruth spat on to the small square of brown carpet.

Mary moved forward, and made another attempt to speak, but Ruth tried to kick her, so she backed away to the door.

'This is one of Ruth's bad days, Mary. She'll be all right in a minute, won't you, Ruth?' Sister Betty was sitting on top of Ruth in the armchair. Ruth struggled to get free, like a large dog being held too tightly by a loving child.

'The pills are beginning to take effect; she'll be all right.' Ruth had given up struggling, and settled for sobbing. The sobs sounded like water being let out of a large bath.

'I'm sorry, Mary. We didn't know you were in here, or I would have taken Ruth to her room. You go for your walk now, while it's fine.' Mary opened the door, and left the room. In the corridor, she asked a nurse what was wrong with Ruth, but all the nurse said was that this was one of Ruth's bad days, and that she had one every other week.

Ruth was not to be seen at lunch-time, but after tea Mary walked into the lounge, and saw her sitting cross-legged in one of the corners, her face to the wall. Mary placed a hand gently on Ruth's shoulder, but Ruth spun round, and growled, 'You!' The word 'You' carried so much contempt and hatred that Mary wanted to go upstairs and cry on her bed, but instead she moved to the other side of the lounge, and pretended to read a copy of *Woman*. The desire to explain to Ruth that she was innocent and the longing to know what had gone wrong kept making her want to shout 'Why?' as loud as she could, but Mary knew that if she did this it would be as bad as throwing two vases of flowers at the wall, so she continued pretending to read, all the time feeling Ruth's eyes on her.

Later, in the Television Room, Ruth knelt, sucking her thumb, her head on someone else's lap, and by bed-time the nurses had moved Ruth's belongings out of the room in which Mary slept.

In the morning, after breakfast, Mary packed her bundle, polished her new shoes, and made sure that Sister Betty was busy in her office, before walking to the Main Gate, and through it onto the country road.

On the bus that was taking her to the centre of London, Albert remarked that she was well out of it, and Mary felt forced to agree.

# A SECOND HONEYMOON

Mary had found some string. Quite a lot. It was that nice soft sort. Pulling at it, she tested its strength. Some string you couldn't trust nowadays; it would let you down just when you needed support. But this was her favourite kind. Held to her nose, and stretched at arm's length, it measured six yards. It was very nice string, much more than she needed. Three yards was the most she would need for her bundle, and that would go round double.

'I'll cut it in half, and save the other half for emergencies. String doesn't weigh much, after all.' This was one of the most important and difficult problems for Mary, what to save, and what to throw away. She constantly had to make snap decisions, and often regretted them later. The decisions to be made this morning were far too important to be snapped.

Seven days ago, she had woken with a desire to go to Fleetwood, where she and Albert had spent their honeymoon, and today was the day she had chosen to start her journey.

'Please don't rain today.' Mary wished very hard that it wouldn't rain today.

Picking up her bundle to make sure yet again that it was not too heavy, she slung it across her back, and walked up and down.

'It's surprising how small things that weigh nothing, add up when you put them together.' Again she put it down. It was not too heavy.

She was excited, that's what it was. Excitement. She had always loved going on holiday, and this in a sense was a holiday. Starting out on a journey was exciting too.

Mary had been living in her luxury flat on the building site for five months now. She had soon settled into her old routine, walking during the day, and coming back to the flat to talk to Albert when the men had finished work. Nobody had pursued her from the hospital or the place in the country. And she was glad that she had told no one, not even Ruth, about her luxury flat.

Around Christmas time, it had become very cold on the third floor, and she had been forced to move down to the ground floor, where there was less wind, and cover herself with old cement-bags. But as soon as the weather had started to get warmer she had moved up to the third floor again, where she could survey the site.

One thing worried her. And it had to be said. 'Say it out loud, girl. Get it off your chest,' Albert would say. 'It's never as bad, once you've put a name to it.' Mary had put a name to it several times, and said it out loud over and over again, and it still worried her. She tried saying it out loud once more for good luck. 'Will I be able to come back here?'

It was true that they showed no signs of finishing the Luxury Flats With Shops And Parking Area. The notice had said 'FOURTEEN STORIES', and every day Mary counted the windows from the top downwards, and it was still only five. She had started to believe that they had stopped work here, been called away to another job perhaps. Several things hadn't moved for some days now, and the piles of sand grew neither smaller nor bigger.

There was no telling how long she would be away, of course. Her holiday might take weeks. If they came back to work while she was away, and changed the fence round the building site, then where would she be? Or they might just find the two loose planks and nail them down tighter, so that she was unable to get through them. She would hate to lose this home. She felt safe here, and it was dry.

The bundle had been tied with the soft white string. It was very neatly done, and there was a large loop for slinging it over her shoulder. She looked up at the sky again. The sun had come out from behind a cloud, and it was clear that there would be no rain today. Mary moved to where the door would be. Oh yes, there was still a great deal to be done before they could have real luxury flats here. She started down the three flights of concrete stairs. These would have carpet on, but not for a good while yet. On the ground floor was a pile of steel window-frames. Three weeks ago, Mary had taken a screw from the floor, and scratched a cross on the top one. It was still there. Before stepping out into the daylight, and crossing the ditches and pipes ('Haven't done the plumbing yet') she did her usual check from the window to make sure no one was about. At the fence, she pushed the planks out slowly, looked right, left and right again, stepped out, and quickly put them back into position. The large billboard at the front of the site still said 'FOURTEEN STORIES'.

Never start a journey on an empty stomach, so breakfast was the next important thing. Mary's stomach felt strange. 'Butterflies', they called that. It was the excitement; after all, she was leaving home.

The S.K.R. (or 'South Kensington Restaurant', to give it its full name) is really a cafeteria, and opens at seven thirty a.m. Mary was the first person served this morning, and was therefore able to sit in what she considered the best corner, which is the one to the left of the door as you enter. From there she could see the whole of the rest of the café. At that time of the morning, the tea is freshly made, and the toast hot. Mary nibbled at her slice of toast, making it last, always with one hand on her cup in case anyone should try to clear it away before she had finished. The disadvantage of eating in the morning is that there are never any newspapers left on the tables. Yesterday's have been cleared away, and today's haven't been read yet.

'The Edgware Road is what you want if you're going up north. Starts at Marble Arch, and goes all the way to Edgware; hence its name. When you get to Edgware, you're as good as there, aren't you?' He had laughed. Mary had wondered why he had laughed. He was a nice man, very helpful, but he didn't know much about Fleetwood; it was a long way past Edgware. Still, he had been very definite about the Edgware Road's going north.

Next to the cash-desk was a little window-sill. Mary noticed, for the first time, a tumbler containing paper napkins. Very few people ever took one. There they sat, neatly folded cone shapes, at least twenty or thirty. Mary wanted some, and her want was strong. She had a use for them. She could go over and take one or two, but that would mean leaving her tea unattended, and if she carried her cup with her, that would attract too much attention, because it was rude manners to carry your food around while you were eating. The S.K.R. was filling up now. People on their way to work were coming in for breakfast, but still no one seemed very interested in the paper napkins. Perhaps people take them more with their lunch; after all, you don't really need one unless you're wearing your best dress or trousers.

It had come to her what she must do. When she had finished, she would walk over to the tumbler, and take two – perhaps three if she could. She would pretend to wipe her mouth and hands on them as she left. Then, when outside, she would stuff them in her pocket. Marble Arch was easy to get to. It wasn't far, just through the park. Going through Hyde Park would be nice, because the sun had come out again. That was another good thing about sitting in the best corner. From there, one could see a patch of sky. The patch was blue, just enough to make a pair of bellbottoms for a thin sailor. The newspaper which the man at the next table was reading said that it was April the third. Summer was coming. She would get a sun-tan, swim in the sea, and watch the boats go to the Isle of Man.

Absent-mindedly she had drunk the mouthful of tea she was saving to hold. The cup was empty; there weren't even any tea-leaves at the bottom. What do they do with tea-leaves nowadays? She had once had her fortune told by them. But none of it had come true, so maybe it was a good thing that one didn't get tea-leaves any more.

Mary got up, and walked over to the paper napkins. Before taking one, she licked her lips and looked at her hands, to show anyone who might be watching what she was going to do and why. Reaching out and taking what she thought to be two, she saw some pink ones hidden between the white ones. They were such a pretty colour, and she had never seen pink ones before. She wanted to put back the two white, and take two pink, but the ones in her hand had been marked by the licked fingers. Panicking, she took the lot. Coming out of the cafeteria more quickly than she would normally have done, she heard, 'Well, really! Did you see that? Not content with sitting there daydreaming for an hour! Will you fetch some more, and I'll fold them? No, just the white ones.'

Mary headed for Hyde Park, up Exhibition Road, past the Victoria and Albert Museum. Albert had christened it 'Mary and Albert's Museum', and they had intended to go and have a look inside it one day, but never did. Inside the park, each gust of wind blew down a new layer of horse-chestnut blossom. It covered the ground like snow. Mary tried to make footprints in it, but the blossom sprang back into position, and refused to melt. Scooping some up in her hands, she studied the little pink centre of each flower. There were hundreds of them, and up in the tree, thousands more. Then there were all the other trees – millions of tiny pink centres, and millions of creamy off-white petals.

Crossing the road that runs thrugh the park is difficult at that time of the morning. She stood for a long time, watching the evenly spaced cars glide along. At last there was a small gap, just enough for her to do a quick dash. The bundle bounced about on her back. At the other side, she tied another three knots in the string, and made it tight. This was good-quality string. It wouldn't let her down.

At Marble Arch, she crossed the road by the underpass, and, after several tries, found the Edgware Road. Pacing out the flagstones, she sang out loud, 'If you tread on a nick you'll marry a brick, and a snail will dance at your wedding.' Mary wondered if any snails had danced at her own wedding. She supposed not. They weren't easy to come by in the middle of Preston. They needed soil, and apart from a potted palm at the Chinese Restaurant where the reception had been held, she didn't remember seeing any. She would make it a point to look out for snails on her way. 'I suppose it's just a saying, and they don't dance at all. Unless *they're* getting married. I suppose, when they do marry, there's a squabble which house to live in.' Mary gripped tight to the string which tied her home to her back, and decided to think of something else. On the other side of the road was a shop that called itself 'Green With Envy', but everything in the window was red and white. The signs said 'A5 AND THE NORTH'. At the Kilburn High Road Essoldo, she crossed the street and sat on the steps, looking at the pictures outside. Removing her shoes, she found the beginnings of a blister. The film on show was called *Mission Impossible*.

The Save-Up Supermarket in the Kilburn High Road was a

new venture, and its Manager, Alfred Lane Banks, was also new. His previous job had been to sell insurance door-to-door, but advancement was slow, and the gambler in his nature could be thwarted no longer. Added to that, he had read a book called *Sell*, an American publication, singing the praises of colourful open display and canned music. He had also read a book about a famous confidence trickster, so he had lied in his letter of application, stating that he had toured America, studying methods of sale there. He had quoted a few names of chain-stores and directors of large companies, added such advertising phrases as 'finding the product's sex appeal' (all gleaned from *Sell*), and, since none of the directors of Save-Up Supermarkets had read or even heard of the book, they had been greatly impressed. When asked for references, he wrote back saying that they had been so flattering that he had got embarrassed and torn them up.

He was engaged, and in turn set about engaging a staff. Since he had no experience of this, he followed one of the book's Golden Rules to the letter. The rule was 'Go For Youth'. All the staff, with the exception of the cleaner, tended therefore to be school-leavers.

Another of the Golden Rules of *Sell* was to carry as large and varied a range of stock as one has room for. Carried away by enthusiasm and the free hand he was being given by the owners of Save-Up, Alfred had in his first week ordered too much of everything, and even flouted the policy of Save-Up by ordering fifteen pounds of black olives. When the stock arrived (as it seemed to every minute of the day), Alfred filled the shelves, the window, the Stock Room, the back yard, the aisle between the shelves, and his Ford Cortina. A small flat area was found on the roof, but only a limited amount of food could be put up there for fear of pigeons. The customers stepped cautiously over boxes of melting frozen peas (since the deep-freeze was full of every flavour of mousse), and made their way to where they thought the Cash Desk would be – the young cashier being hidden by plastic buckets given free with every purchase over one pound. She had been given this job, not because mental arithmetic was her best subject, but because, once engaged, she had explained that she had bad feet, and this was a job in which she could sit down. In order to make it possible for customers to get at the twenty-seven different varieties of washing powder, Alfred lined up some of the stock outside the shop. This was brought in again last thing at night, and he would arrive an hour before the shop opened in the morning, in order to clear a passage through the shelves for his employees to reach the Wash Room.

Mary carefully walked round the ironing boards and boxes of Andrex Toilet Rolls that jutted out on to the pavement. From inside the Supermarket, the Flower-Pot Men could be heard singing 'If you're going to San Francisco, wear some flowers in your hair.' She liked the song so much that she stopped and pretended to read the colourful posters on display in the window. They advertised 'Powdered Mashed Potatoes that he'll love you for', 'Give Him Ideas, with a tin of cut-price Passion Fruit: Large Size Half the Price', 'The Frozen Fish Supper that Goes with ANYTHING'.

As Mary turned from the window to continue her journey, the bundle on her back brushed against some of the ironing boards, which in turn knocked down a large pyramid of toilet rolls. The colourful open display rolled about all over the street. Kilburn High Road became a sea of Misty Blue, Blush Pink, Fern Green and Primrose Yellow streamers. Twin Packs were split into single rolls under the wheels of cars. Some cars stopped dead, and others tried to get round them. A spotted Dalmatian jumped out of a car window, barking, and chased a roll of Blush Pink along the gutter.

Alfred ran from the shop. He had had the foresight to

bring a cardboard box with him, and now darted in and out of the hooting traffic picking up his stock. The wind propelled the two-ply luxury toilet tissue along. 'Miss O'Grady!' Alfred shouted back into the shop. A mini-skirted girl in high heels hobbled out into the street. This caused almost as much attention as the toilet rolls, for each time she bent down to pick one up she would give a pull at her inadequate skirt.

The cars hooted louder. Two bus drivers leaned from their cabs, and shouted 'Bring on more dancing girls.' Mary stood fascinated. A small boy suddenly ran from another shop into the road, shouting 'Lavvy paper! Lavvy paper!' Mary caught his arm, and swung him round, back on to the pavement. Landing on his knees, he let out an ear-splitting scream. The ungrateful mother pulled the boy away from Mary with a look of pure hatred.

Slowly the traffic started to move again. The lady whose Dalmatian had disappeared up a side street had abandoned her white Rover to look for it, and a smiling policeman climbed into the driver's seat and tried to find first gear. Alfred stood outside his shop beside Mary, with a box of battered toilet rolls. Sweat ran down his face, and he felt his underpants and vest sticking to him. He had promised the policeman that he would pick up more of the paper, and Miss O'Grady had promised she would go and see *Mission Impossible* with the policeman. Alfred picked up the card that read 'Special Offer. Twin Pack 1/6'. Sixty twin packs of Andrex at one and sixpence a pack. He did the sum on the back of the card, and added a note, 'Used for Demonstration Purposes'.

# 'I LOVE MARY'

Mary spread herself out on the grass, and squinted up at the sun. She was so pleased that she'd decided to come up north. Tomorrow she would be in Fleetwood. She knew exactly what she was going to do when she got there, and in what order. First she would walk through the covered market, smell the fish, and buy herself a pair of kippers for supper. Second, watch a boat arrive from the Isle of Man. Third, walk through the gardens, and look at the floral clock. Fourth and last, go and see the motorbike racing.

Lying next to Albert at Number Seven, Priory Road, and listening to the motorbikes go whizzing round the track. Then the announcement over the loud-speaker declaring the winner. Hours would pass, while they lay side by side, naked and just touching. Albert would move his broad dry hand down the centre of her body, and stroke the underside of each of her breasts in turn with the back of his fingers, as if painting a picture. Slowly, and trying hard not to cry out, but always with a murmur of delight, she would move very slightly away. Then he would rest the palm of his hand on her belly, and leave it there. As if for ever, it stayed there. For ages and ages, he would not move it, the warm dry hand with the fingers spread, until she, unable to bear it, parted her legs. Mary would count ten slowly. It nearly always came to ten before he slid hard fingers between her open legs. Then she felt free to move towards him, always whispering, 'No.' Always he kissed her 'No' away, his fingers working to release her juices. Always he put his leg between hers, and always as he moved himself up inside her, he said 'I love Mary,' and the motorbikes would roar round and round the cinder track, revving and revving, while Albert rode up and down on Mary, his hands round her buttocks, holding them apart.

Mary spread herself, and listened to the result of the final race. She wanted him to bite her, but dared not ask. Albert rode on. He was very good at making love, for he could make it last as long as he wanted before exercising his iron control, and although Mary knew nothing of other men's bodies, she guessed that Albert was well equipped; he had once joked that it was his most prominent feature. Mary giggled in the grass. It smelled very nice. The sun, and the bird song, and the various insect noises made her drowsy. She became aware that her hand was inside her knickers, and that she was playing with herself. She was mildly shocked, but since nobody was about, she decided to leave it there, and with this decision fell asleep.

It was the middle of the school holidays, and Alan Norton, aged fifteen, had been bored all day. He had been sacked from his paper-round for making an improper suggestion to the newsagent's wife. He said that she had made the suggestion first, but either way he got the sack. The nearest cinema was four miles away. There he and his three mates would find some high-school girls to chat up.

They all had bicycles, and the evening was light and warm. 'What's on?' 'I dunno. Who cares? I don't go to watch the picture anyway.' 'Will Christine be there?' 'If she's not, there'll be someone else. I might even let *you* have a lick of it.'

They zigzagged across the country lane. Alan either had the fastest bike or the most energy, for he led the way, and

hadn't fallen asleep. If only she had hidden herself on the other side of the hedge. How could she have thought it was Albert come back to her?

'I didn't enjoy it, Albert.' Albert did not reply.

'I dreamed it was you.' No reply.

'Did you watch them, Albert?' No reply.

'I know you couldn't stop it. Being dead.' No reply.

'Are you there, Albert?' No reply. Mary tried to visualize his face, but couldn't. Slowly she realized that Albert had left her.

Mary had never in her life been as unhappy as this. The total feeling of despair frightened and at the same time fascinated her. Without thinking why, she rose to her feet, pulled at her bundle, threw it over her shoulder, and moved across the fields away from the village towards which the boys had ridden.

Albert had always been angry if another man so much as looked at her, not that many had. It was an accident; she hadn't known. No other man had ever touched her besides Albert – Albert and a boy young enough to be her son. He had called her names, and lost his iron control, spilling his seeds inside her. Now the seeds would germinate, and grow into a little thing. She could still feel the pushing and hurting as he had bounced about on top of her. His best feature had been more prominent than Albert's.

Perhaps when she had had a pee, the soreness would go away. Mary found a bush, and tried, but nothing happened.

Without knowing where she was going, she moved on, walking quickly, sobbing and talking out loud to Albert, justifying herself for having slept. She had never done it before. To lie on the grass verge in broad daylight was unforgivable.

Trying to cross a stream on stepping-stones, she slipped twice, and gave up. Mary sat on the sharp pebbles that formed the bottom of the stream, with water up to her waist. She tried to open herself, and wash out the sticky white seeds, but the cold made her tight and numb. Forcing her legs apart, she stretched herself open until she was able to splash in the icy water.

How could she have dreamed it was Albert? He had never loved her like that. She had wanted him so much. Now she needed him. More than ever. If only he would say something.

Standing up in the stream, she shouted at a tree, 'Come back, please. I can explain. Please, Albert, say something. You're the only one I can talk to. Talk to me. Please!' But the tree remained a tree. Mary looked around her. There was nobody else there. Albert might be hiding, making up his mind whether or not to come. He had always needed time for decisions of this nature. Perhaps if she waited.

Mary dragged herself out of the water, and sank down on the grass. It was beginning to get dark. Studying her wet shoes, she thought how water ruins the leather. 'They don't last when they've been got wet.' In her bundle was a newspaper. She would stuff them with that, and dry them out.

Mary's stomach made a noise. 'He's given me a baby.' There was no doubt; she could feel it. The roundness. Already it was growing. Mary lay on her back, and stretched out, feeling the pains of childbirth. To help the baby's progress, she pushed at her upper stomach with her hands. The sky was becoming a darker grey. Screwing her eyes up in agony, Mary imagined the seeds, not yet an hour planted, bursting forth into unexpected life. Not a skinny screaming bit of life, but a chubby cherub, who would arrive wearing his own nappies.

Mary pushed and strained again, but nothing happened. 'I hope he's not too chubby, or he won't be able to get out.' She was very tired, and she was lying on damp grass. 'Can't stay here. It's damp. Must get up. Don't come yet, baby, please.'

Mary balanced herself carefully, and tried to walk. But this was more difficult with stomach pushed forward and shoulders back. By walking round in a circle, she tested her strength. No, it was not going to be easy. And what about her bundle? She mustn't carry heavy weights. What was more, she couldn't stay out in the middle of this field all night. Cows have their babies in fields, but they're used to it. The cherub would want to drink from her boobs; that's what they did. Would it be painful? Albert had often pretended to, and that had thrilled her.

It was getting cold as well as dark. Mary walked round again, trying to get used to this odd leaning-backwards feeling. She wanted very much to pick up her belongings, but dared not. 'Catch Albert getting caught out like that! Lying on a grass verge in broad daylight.' Challenged by that thought, she bent down slowly, and just as slowly lifted her bundle. How could she know she was doing the right thing? Usually Albert told her. Tears again. Twice in one day. She couldn't look after herself, let alone a 'little thing'. She didn't know how. It might die, and they would blame her, and lock her up. Cherubs were too small and slippery. She might drop it. It might cry.

Mary stopped crying. A thought had occurred to her. She must persuade the baby not to come. Albert had told her of ways he'd heard of not having a baby if you thought you were going to. There were dangerous things that some women had to do, but what were they? One of them was something to do with knitting-needles, but what? Gin; that was it. You had to drink a gallon of gin. 'But gin makes me sick, and a gallon is a lot to have to drink.' There was something else. What was it? Hot baths. A very hot bath made baby decide not to come. But it had to be as hot as you could bear.

She could have a hot bath the moment she arrived in Fleetwood. They had the U.D.C. Baths there. She and Albert knew them well. That would tell the 'little thing' not to come, and it would go back to Heaven, or wherever cherubs came from.

A hot bath cost sixpence. Perhaps more now. And maybe she should have two, in case baby didn't understand the first time. Mary had spend her pound for the week. She remembered the half-crown she had thrown into the ditch. 'We'd better go back, baby, and get it.'

Quickly but carefully she made her way across the fields, hoping that there would be light enough to see when she got there. When she had crossed two fields, Mary farted loudly, and the pain and roundness in her stomach disappeared. Perhaps in Fleetwood, Albert would come back to her.

Something made a noise, and Mary stopped. Then it happened again. It came from somewhere in front of her. Mary turned, ready to forget her stomach and the half-crown, and run the other way. Then the noise came again, louder and quite distinct. It said, 'Help.'

It was the boys, come back to play games with her. Mary stood, frozen to the spot. The voice was now behind her.

'Over here, quickly.'

A wood-pigeon rose from the grass ahead of her, causing her to let out a yell.

'Please, it's me. Over here, behind this bush.'

Mary started slowly to move away. She must be careful. There had been four of them; they would surround her.

'For pity's sake, help me, whoever you are. I know you're there. I'll die if you leave me. I've lost too much blood. I can't get to ... feel ... my feet.'

The voice was not that of a boy, but a man, and the man was crying.

'Who are you? I'll get the police if you've come to play games.'

The man shouted back that his name was Jim Gibbons, and he was caught in a fox-trap. Mary moved towards the bush slowly, and saw the lower half of a man's body with what looked like a piece of farm machinery attached to one of the legs.

'It's a bloody trap. Do you think you can get it off?' His voice was weaker now.

Mary looked down at the two half-circles of jagged rusty teeth which were sticking into the man's leg. Raw bits of flesh hung out of the torn trouser, and a fly walked round the edge of the tear.

'I made it worse when I fell. It digs deeper every time I move. If you can lift my leg, and pull the two blades apart, you might be able to get it off.' Mary turned her head away. 'You must try. I've been here all day, and the longer it's there, the more harm it's doing. Wait until I go unconscious again; I keep doing that. Then do as I told you.' With an effort to rise that caused him some pain, he grabbed and held her hand. 'When you get it off, wrap it in something. You've got some rags there.' He pointed to Mary's bundle. 'Then run over to the houses – over there about a mile – and tell them to fetch the ambulance quickly. Here! You may need this.' He reached into his inside pocket with the utmost care, and took a card from it. Mary looked at the neatly printed card, which read 'JAMES F. GIBBONS. 9, HENNEL LANE, WROXTON. HIGH-CLASS FAMILY BUTCHER'.

'You will get it off, won't you?'

When the man loosened his grip on her hand, Mary realized that it was because he had fainted. The first thing to do was to rip away most of his trouser-leg so as to see what she was doing. The rusty teeth had buried themselves in his flesh just above the ankle, and the twisting and turning he had done while in pain, plus the fall, had scraped a good deal of flesh from the bone.

Lifting his leg was easy, though it started the bleeding again. Mary bit hard into her bottom lip, to force down her almost overwhelming urge to be sick. Since the sweat on her hands made gripping the rusty blades difficult, she lifted the front of her dress over the man's legs, and used it to hold the trap. But it was no good. No matter how hard she strained, she could not even move the blades, let alone part them enough to get them over the man's foot. Finally she gave up, wrapping his leg in a cotton dress from her bundle, and made her way across the fields in the direction towards which he had pointed.

As they worked to free the trapped butcher, one of the ambulance men said to Mary that this was a home-made fox trap, and that the R.S.P.C.A. had fought hard, and finally managed to make them illegal. The man's companion laughed, and said that he knew at least three farmers who still used them. When told by Mary that he should report them, he asked how he would set about proving it.

One of the two men asked the other what he thought the butcher was doing out here in the middle of the fields. Mary lifted a bag which had been lying underneath the trapped man, and several specimens of wild flowers fell on to the grass.

The ambulance men had taken ten shillings from the man's pockets as he lay on the stretcher, and given them to Mary. They would be passing the main Fleetwood road, and would drop her off, since two minutes here or there would make no difference to their patient, who was now unconscious.

In searching for half a crown, Mary had found ten shillings. So her profit on the entire afternoon was seven and six.

# FLEETWOOD

It was Sunday. She had arrived, and it was Sunday. The sign said 'FLEETWOOD'. There were tram-lines still, and trams (though not many today). Mary stood still, and asked Albert if he was there, but he made no reply. Perhaps, when he saw her visiting their favourite places, he would relent and forgive her.

She walked on towards the sea-front. There were small changes; one or two shops looked new. But the houses were the same. Mary felt cheated. Nothing had happened to her; she didn't feel any different. But she must feel different; this was Fleetwood. Mary almost walked all the way back to the edge of the town, to the sign that said 'FLEETWOOD', so that she could pass it again. She had expected that when she entered the town, thousands of memories would come flooding back, so many that she would have to stand still and try not to think too fast, so that she could savour them all fully. But she remembered nothing, except that this was how Fleetwood looked and where everything was.

With Albert she had noticed things. Simply by glancing at a piece of wall as they passed, she would feel she knew how many bricks were in it, and the reason why the wall was there. While they sat on a bench, she would pick out a flag-stone to study. She knew how it felt without touching it. If it was wet or covered in moss, it was like that because that was how it liked to be.

There had been a shop in Lexham Street where she and

Albert had pawned their best shoes, but the only shop in Lexham Street now was a Cut-Price Emporium. Mary wandered inside, and was immediately conscious of being watched. A large sales-lady was explaining to a young man the various merits of Fibre Glass Curtaining. It was a stiff ugly fabric, which needed no ironing.

Mary looked around. This couldn't be the same little shop they had stood outside for hours, with their shoes wrapped in newspaper like fish and chips. Now bored women stood dreaming behind stalls of cheap tea-towels and elastic swimming-trunks. The large lady's eyes followed Mary round the shop, but she continued talking to the embarrassed young man. There was nothing here to remind Mary of the little man they had bargained with, and his little green tickets which read 'HENRY DUCKWORTH. ALWAYS FAIR ALWAYS HONEST. 7 AUG 46. ONE SHILLING AND NINE PENCE'.

'Can I help you, love?' The large lady was barring Mary's way.

'No, thank you. I'm just looking round.'

'That's all right then, love. Feel free.'

The young man had taken his advantage, and was making for the door with all decent speed, but the large lady was more experienced than he in this kind of game. 'I haven't shown you our shuttle.' She threw her voice towards him with the skill of somebody catching butterflies. He didn't even flutter. He turned, and was caught.

Hanging from the ceiling was a perfectly ordinary shuttle. 'It was given me by one of the local mills before they closed down. I think it's disgusting, don't you?' The young man nodded, to show that he was ready to be put on a pin and mounted. 'The amount of foreign muck they import into this country! Calling it fabric! It's a travesty.' Counting the money in his pocket, he agreed. 'I won't touch it, you know. I always ask where it's been before I'll put my hands to it.

Feel that.' The young man felt the stiff ugly fabric, and bought five yards of it. Mary left the shop, as he paid with money from his wallet. 'That's right, love. Let the moths out.'

The Original Kipper Shop displayed its salty wares, offering to send them to any part of the world – where many an aunt might delight to see them squeezed through her letter-box. The day was very windy, but nevertheless, hardy men and women sat facing out to sea, and battled to open their copies of the *News of the World* while Sunday lunch was being prepared. Others queued at a small kiosk, and settled for a less energetic read, such as *True Crime*, *Love Digest* or *Men, the Mafia Run Our Prisons*.

Mary had in her head a list of things to do and places to visit. Some of the things on the list could not be done today, because it was Sunday. In her mind, the list had an order:

1st. Visit Covered Market, and talk to Albert.

2nd. Watch a boat arrive from the Isle of Man, and talk to Albert.

3rd. Walk through Gardens, look at Floral Clock, and talk to Albert.

4th. Go down Priory Road, and talk to Albert.

5th. Visit Motorbike Racing, and talk to Albert.

The pawn shop would have had third place on the list, but she had passed where it should have been, and had stopped. She was not surprised that Albert had not spoken to her there, because it had changed so much, and he would not have liked being overheard by the woman who ran it. If Mary kept talking to him, he would come round, and return to her. After all, they were in Fleetwood again.

The Covered Market did not open on a Sunday, and Mary could not find out at what time the Ferry Boat arrived from the Isle of Man, if indeed it arrived at all on Sunday. Walking through the gardens of the Floral Hall, and gazing at the

Floral Clock, Mary talked to Albert about the flowers and the people she could see, about the weather, about her plans, and about all that had happened to her since she had last heard his voice (leaving out the episode of the boy who had spilled his seed inside her). At the end of every little speech, she would coax Albert with a question, always asking a different one, so that there was more chance of its getting an answer. 'What did you have for breakfast this morning?' Albert didn't reply. 'Do you like the colour of that dress? The one the lady sitting next to me is wearing.' The lady sitting next to Mary got up and moved, but Albert didn't reply. 'Do they wear dresses where you are, and don't say you haven't noticed?' Albert didn't reply. 'Have you seen any butterflies there?' Albert didn't reply.

Priory Road is like many other roads in Fleetwood, but Mary found it almost without thinking. Number Seven had a lilac front door, and Mary was angry that she couldn't remember what colour it had been when they had spent their honeymoon there. She leaned against the window, and peered into the dimly lit room. 'I'll bet you can remember what colour that front door was, can't you?' Albert didn't reply.

In one of the corners of the room, Tarzan climbed a tree and swung out over the jungle, stretching his over-developed muscles. 'Are you watching your weight? I expect you've noticed how much slimmer I am.' Albert didn't reply. Suddenly another face appeared on the other side of the window, and, but for the glass, would have pressed against Mary's. A pale, hostile face, with fly-away glasses and blue hair. Its eyes narrowed, magnified by the glasses, its lips tightened, and the curtains swished across the window.

The Motorbike Stadium now belonged to the Fleetwood Football Club. The gate was open, and Mary walked round the bench seats so as not to cross the pitch. On the opposite side of the field a man wearing a flat cap against the sun sat

on a beer crate, and filled in with white paint the large letters
he had traced out faintly in chalk. Mary asked the man what
had happened to the motorbikes, and he explained without
looking up that they had been 'taken off' three years ago. The
man looked and sounded depressed, so Mary read aloud what
he had written: 'SELLING SCRAP METAL? THEN CONTACT J.
HOLMSTROM, KNOT END.'

This brought no reaction, so Mary moved away and sat on
one of the benches. Looking at the green turf and rows of
empty seats, she tried to imagine the cinders and the loud-
speaker that crackled. 'Do you remember the motorbikes and
that loudspeaker that crackled?' Albert didn't reply. 'Can't
you even say Yes or No?' Albert didn't reply. 'Please, Albert,
I beg you. I don't want to cry any more. Please say you'll come
soon. You know I've never loved anyone else. You have all my
love, Albert. Please accept it.' Albert didn't reply.

Mary spent the night in a field a mile outside Fleetwood.
Next morning she made her way to the Covered Market. She
was early, and the stalls were still being set out with things
for sale. Mary moved between the chatting stallholders, who
exchanged gossip about the weekend, or where they were
going for their holidays. 'I'd like to get him to Spain this year,
but his ulcer won't allow it. It's always been an ambition of
mine to see a bull killed in the ring.'

This at least hadn't changed. The noise and smell (mainly
fish) were as she had remembered, and so were the straight
rows of stalls and the boys with trolley trucks unloading
lorries and steering the trolleys quickly in and out of the
early shoppers. Mary visited five fish stalls, and then returned
to the first. Looking at the hundreds of kippers, she asked
Albert which pair she should buy. 'If you were buying yourself some kippers, Albert, which pair would you choose?'
Albert didn't reply. She stood in front of the stall for another
five minutes, in case he should change his mind, and then

bought the pair on top of the pile. By buying them, she had overspent her budget, but they would last two days, and be a change from meat pies.

While waiting for the Isle of Man ferry, Mary studied the Town Guide, which was a map that could be rolled up or down, depending on whether your interest lay north or south. Around it were cards which advertised Hair Styles by Henri, 'Belle Madame' with Bernard, the Dogs' Beauty Shop and Boutique, the Happy Cheese Restaurant of High Quality, Sauna Baths, and Where to apply for Space in This Guide. Again Mary spoke to Albert. 'What shall I go and see after I've met the ferry?' Albert didn't reply.

The ferry unloaded its few passengers and little cargo. Two women of Mary's age, wearing trousers and matching white sweaters, both with their hair tightly permed, walked hand in hand up to the window and bought tickets for the return trip to the island. Mary asked Albert to guess how long the journey took, but he didn't answer.

Their favourite Amusement Arcade was still there, but the pin-ball machine had been replaced by one-armed bandits. Most of the arcade was taken up by a Bingo Stall, at which seven women sat, with five or six cards apiece. The cards had little shutters with which to cover the numbers when called, and numbered ping-pong balls were groped from a green velvet bag by a spotty youth. The conversation between games (for there was none during play) was mainly to do with one of the women, who had covered the rollers in her hair with a chiffon headscarf. This woman had no eyebrows.

'Well, I shaved them off last night like it said in *Woman*, and put this cream on to sleep in. Only when I get up this morning, I can't find a pencil to draw them on again, can I?'

'You should have tried with a burnt match.'

'I never thought of that.'

'Eyebrows down for a full house.'

At the end of the Promenade, there was a restaurant run by the Corporation. Blue plastic cups, already set out on tubular steel tables, waited to be filled. Above the door hung the obligatory notice, warning that the consumption of food should be restricted to that purchased on the premises. On the wall, green, red and yellow goldfish pouted out yellow, red and green bubbles. Mary drank a cup of weak tea slowly before walking back to her field. On the way, she ate the first of the two kippers, uncooked. Finally, she asked Albert if there was anything she could do, or stop doing, which might persuade him to talk to her. Albert didn't reply.

The next day was cold, and Mary spent most of it sitting in a shelter and looking out to sea.

The fourth day was cold too, but Mary had made a decision.

Two clocks stood in a wooden frame on the Promenade. One said twenty-three minutes past nine, and the other, twenty-five past eight. Mary wondered why they should disagree, and both be wrong. Beneath the clocks, obscured by bird droppings, were the words 'HIGH TIDE, A.M. AND P.M.'

Small birds hopped about on the pebbles, trying to find their lunch, while Mary ate the remaining kipper. When she had finished, she threw them its head and tail, at which they pecked happily until a large pigeon scared them off. The pigeon was uninterested in kipper, and dragged half a cucumber sandwich behind the rock. Given its location, it might not be a pigeon at all, but a seagull.

A middle-aged couple lay head to toe on two lilos, reading Georgette Heyer. The woman had her shoes off and her dress tucked into her knickers, but she wore a blanket around her shoulders against the cold.

Walking over sand feels good, but one must do it properly. Sitting on the sea-wall to remove her shoes and socks was something that did bring back a memory, if only because of the difference between then and now. They had been Size Four, cherry red with an ankle strap and medium-sized heel. She had worn them through the first week of the honeymoon, and then pawned them for seven shillings to Mr Duckworth. He had admitted that they were a good shoe, and partly handmade. Her stockings had not been very fine, but fine enough to make taking them off a pleasure.

It had taken time, removing her stockings. She remembered the giggling embarrassment of having to feel under her skirt to find those little rubber nipples that hung from her suspender-belt to hold the stockings in place. This had always excited Albert, which was partly why it took so long. The first time she had done it, she had caught sight of him sliding his hand into his trouser pocket. She had deliberately pretended not to be able to get up, so that he had to help her with both his hands, and she could see the front of his trousers stick out. That she could excite him like this pleased her a great deal. Always after that, she would try to delay the putting on or taking off of stockings until Albert was watching.

Mary now wore two and a half pairs of socks. They were not all matching pairs, but the top pair was. She peeled them all off together, and looked at her dirty feet, quickly pushing them under the sand, and rubbing one on top of the other to clean them. She put the socks in her pocket, carried the shoes in one hand, her bundle in the other, and walked forward to the sea.

Partly because of the bundle, but mainly because of not having slept for the last four nights, she was unable to run and dance as she had with Albert. But the sand was there, and the sea was there.

The few holiday-makers, who were braving the wind because they had children and nowhere else to take them, took no notice of the figure in a long coat, walking out to sea.

Mary sat down in the sea, facing Fleetwood, still holding

her shoes and bundle. Now was a good time. If she was going to do it, she could do it now. All she had to do was to lie down, and wait.

She suddenly remembered that she hadn't been on the Pier, but it didn't matter. The salt water bubbled in and out of her openwork shoes, as she held on to them tightly. She could imagine the people putting on one of the many Greens, or sitting round in the Floral Hall making their dogs play with hard rubber balls.

Looking behind her, out to sea, she could just make out the bit of land called Knot End. Ferries still went there, as she had done with Albert. There were lots of places she'd meant to visit, and hadn't. She didn't want to visit anywhere else without Albert. She wanted to find him and explain.

She had been in Fleetwood now for four days, and he had not come. If he didn't come to her in Fleetwood, he would never come. Perhaps he had wanted to come, but couldn't. Anyway it was all the same; she must go to him.

The water came up to her elbows, and was so cold, it made her shiver. All she had to do was to lie down, and wait. This was a good way to find Albert.

A sudden noise made her jump, and swallow some water. It was a curious rounded thing. It skimmed along the top of the water, blowing up a tremendous spray. Along its side were little round windows. Little faces smiled, and little hands waved, and Mary, without thinking, waved back. The swell that it made pushed her about. She tried to get to her feet for balance, but the weight of her wet clothes made standing impossible. Mary crouched as best she could, supporting herself on hands and feet. The little hands waved, and, since she could no longer wave back, she smiled and nodded. Above the windows, Mary read the words 'NOR'WEST HOVERCRAFT'.

When it had gone, the waves settled down, and she sat once more. It was getting dark. Lights were beginning to be switched on. Being alone is one thing; feeling alone is very different. A complete sense of isolation can be the most exciting sensation we ever have. Mary felt 'in control' for the first time in her life. There was the world, and here was she, sitting in the Atlantic Ocean. She had a choice.

Taking a last look at the coastline, she saw Mount Hill and the Floral Clock illuminated. A ship, a rose, two birds in purple and green, and underneath the motto 'ONWARDS' written in petunias. Mary turned, and lowered her back into the water. She had a choice. The water lapped in and out of her ears, and made buzzing noises inside her head. This was a good way. She had made a choice.

After five minutes, Mary opened her eyes. They were above the water. So were her nose and mouth. The tide was going out.

# GIVING UP

Mary walked back to her field through the dark streets, and spent a very cold and sleepless night. It was not until the afternoon of the following day that her clothes finally dried out. All but one thin dress (which she wore) were spread out over the hedge. Some of them had faded, but all of them were clean.

What should she do now? Mary could think of no other form of suicide which didn't involve a great deal of pain. Halfheartedly she looked for toadstools, but could not remember their difference from mushrooms. As a schoolgirl she had collected twenty-seven different kinds of grass, and mounted a sample of each on a large sheet of dark grey paper, with its name printed underneath in capital letters. She had picked mushrooms, and cooked them in milk, delighted by the smell they made. But it didn't matter that now she could not remember what toadstools looked like, or what the grasses and flowers were called (save for one or two of the most common), because there were no toadstools or mushrooms in this field.

Instead there were five hawthorn trees in the middle of Mary's field, standing in line. All but one carried a white blossom. Mary, as usual, searched for birds' nests. On her way to Fleetwood, she had counted thirty-one birds' eggs in various colours, and seven baby birds, recently hatched. She explored the tree without blossom last. Looking up from beneath its branches, she saw that the middle branches were dead. All the branches of all the trees were curved, snarled and spiky, but these were an even odder shape; they had started to go one way, then done a complete turnabout, and grown in several spirals, as if they were trapped inside the other branches, and trying to get out.

The reason was that there were two trees, close together, and one had grown round part of the other. Hawthorns are not parasitical. The healthy tree had gained nothing by the other's death.

In the living branches of the blossomless tree, Mary did find a nest. It contained a dead bird lying over its egg, which was broken and empty. For some reason it had lost most of its feathers, and the back of its head had been eaten away, either by other birds or by a rat.

She had to decide. But there was no hurry. She wandered around the field all day. It was a big field, and she had grown used to walking. Her stride was even. There was no hurry. She would take a walk along one side of the field, then come back to where she had tried to sleep and where the rest of her clothes were drying on the hedge. It was warm. She wore the one thin dress. Her body moved freely under it, and her toes spread themselves to meet the grass. Only the knowledge of having to make up her mind clouded a very pleasant day. She had not really studied her field before, having spent most of her time in Fleetwood. The buttercups and little blue flowers, whose name she didn't know, were pretty.

On one side of the field she discovered a drinking trough, with gnats dancing up and down on its thick green slime. Oddly, it reminded her that she had not eaten today. She was hungry, but she did not feel inclined to walk the mile into Fleetwood, only to find all the shops closed.

Getting ready for bed, she saw that her wedding dress had shrunk, and now had green streaks where it had come into contact with grass and hedge. Since Mary had shrunk a little too, they would probably still fit each other.

Later that night she regretted not having tried to find something to eat. She was unable to get to sleep for hunger. Just after midnight, she ate a handful of grass, chewing it slowly and thoroughly. It tickled the back of her throat, making her cough.

The next morning, Mary walked into Fleetwood, and broke one of her rules by eating two days' allotment of food at one sitting. She could only excuse it by remembering her dip in the sea. Always, as a child, swimming had made her hungry.

At the Post Office, she drew a pound out of her account. She had decided to go back to London. There was nothing else to do.

It was nine thirty a.m. Mary left Fleetwood, and had only reached Blackpool, some nine miles away, by nightfall. It was clear that her journey back was going to take a long time, for her heart was not in it. However, there was no hurry.

The sea-side town was quieter than she had ever known it. The only people to be seen on the beach for the last half-hour of the sun were a man being pulled along by his Alsatian and two courting couples. Since the sun was going down, and Mary knew Blackpool to be a big town, too big to get out of before it got completely dark, there was the problem of finding somewhere to sleep.

Her first thought was to try under one of the piers. After all, there were three to choose from. Being close to North Pier, she tried that first, then Central Pier, and finally South Pier. Since there was still entertainment of a kind happening on all of them, it was difficult to tell which, if any, was suitable, for she did not know at what time the entertainment would stop. Mary sat under each pier in turn, and listened to the noise. Each time, it surrounded her, making her feel as though she were in the room with it. The first noise was by far the most pleasant. A small orchestra played Selections from The Desert Song. But after Where My Caravan Has Rested and a solo from the Red Shadow, the Interval arrived, and the sound of people moving about to find ice cream made Mary wonder what was being offered at the next pier.

A girl sang *Hello, Dolly*, and *Mame*, and tap-danced, and did something which Mary assumed to be three cartwheels, landing heavily. After that, a gentleman from the audience was given a prize for being able to produce a pair of yellow braces. The applause and foot-stamping was so great at this that Mary moved on.

She didn't reach South Pier. She could hear its noise from a considerable distance. She sat some way from the pier, her hands over her ears. She had tired herself out by walking the full length of the Promenade, and needed a short rest, but this was not a problem which could be solved by staying where she was. The high-pitched whine of the electric guitar fizzed under Mary's scalp, and set her teeth on edge. The only solution was to return to *The Desert Song*.

Between Central and North Piers, opposite the Imperial Hotel and under the Main Promenade, there is a glass-fronted public verandah which looks out to sea. It is almost always warm, and has a wooden lattice-work seat along its entire length. The length is the most surprising thing about it – perhaps an eighth of a mile – and the perspective is so perfect as to make the observer seem unreal. It is a glass-sided summer-house, stretched like spaghetti into a perfectly straight line, overlooking the sea. Children race each other from one end to the other, starting the size of a thumb, and growing according to their speed. As they shout, the echo overlaps their yells, making a crowd out of two friends. Sometimes they play with the echo, trying to cheat it by talking too fast, or whispering behind their hands. But even the quietest sound is magnified and made beautiful by this pleasing building.

To Mary, when she found it, it just seemed like an over-large bus shelter. As she entered, it echoed to the sound of her feet, and when she collapsed, sighing, onto the incredibly long bench, it sighed too, only louder, making her look round sharply, and examine the space under the seat. There was no one else there. There were puddles of something on the floor, and a large amount of broken glass, but it was warm and quiet, and she was alone.

Lying full length on the lattice-work bench, her head on her bundle, Mary sighed again in order to listen to the echo. It seemed to last for ever, and sounded so unhappy that she didn't recognize it as the noise she had made. The sea came and went reassuringly, and the sky promised a fine day tomorrow.

At four a.m. she was woken by a young policeman, and told to move on. She had slept, she reckoned, for five hours. It was just light enough to start walking, so she did, passing row upon row of red brick houses, all the same, the same bay windows, embroidered with the same leaded lights. There were leaded lights in the doors too, or occasionally frosted glass, frosted with flowers and leaves and baskets of fruit. Most of the houses were painted different colours, to make a difference, red next door to green, blue semi-detached from lavender, all with little Vacancy Cards saying that they had beds and they had breakfasts.

Mary took her bundle off the right shoulder, and placed it on her left. She was going back to her luxury flat. She had not had a hot bath in Fleetwood, because she had not been able to find the U.D.C. Baths. The cherub had given her no more pain, and so she had been able to forget him. Albert she would not forget. She no longer expected him to speak to her, but she had memories, and she would use them properly.

# PART TWO

■

## PAUL

# ASHES TO ASHES

If Paul happened to see one of Richard's friends coming towards him on the same side of the street, he would try to cross the road so as to avoid a meeting. Often there would be traffic on the road, and Paul would take chances greater than he would ordinarily take, so that drivers would be forced to brake quickly, and would then hoot at him. Paul was convinced that Richard's friend would notice this, and wonder why Paul was trying to avoid him, and perhaps be offended. That would make it all the more necessary to cross the road if Paul were to see him again.

Paul did not dislike Richard's friends, but he could never think of anything to say to them. Worse than that, they never seemed to be able to think of anything to say to him. This had never mattered when Richard was alive, because Richard had thought of things to say, and if Paul had ventured a remark in conversation with any of the friends, Richard, by expanding on it and elaborating it, could make it seem witty, or even wise, and at least not silly. Sometimes Paul had made a witty remark without any help at all, and it had been laughed at.

Conversation on a pavement in South Kensington or Chelsea did not need to be witty or wise, but it did need to keep going, not just emerge, squeezed out word by word, with a growing conviction in both Paul and the friend that neither of them would ever be able to move on. In the old days, when Paul had been walking alone, and had met one of Richard's friends, a smile, or a nod or wave, or a 'Hello, Paul' would have been enough, but that would be heartless now, so soon after Richard's death.

The problem only arose in the street, because Paul did not see Richard's friends at any other time. He had no friends of his own, but had not needed any, since Richard provided all the companionship one could need. There were a great many of Richard's friends, and every Christmas, cards had been sent to them 'With love from Richard and Paul'. None was seen often, but all were seen regularly, at parties, or dinner parties, or occasional weekends with those who had homes in the country. Paul supposed that he ought to go through the Address Book, and write to tell them all that they had lost a friend, but there were too many, and he had never got into the habit of writing letters.

He had not even thought to invite anyone to the cremation, which had been arranged by Richard's solicitor, Mr Freebody. Richard had not been a Christian, so the ceremony had been short and simple. The Director of the crematorium had told Paul that those closest to the deceased liked to read a poem or choose a favourite piece of music, to lend a personal tone to the ceremony, but Paul was a poor sight-reader and Richard's taste in music had been for long orchestral works of no pronounced character to which he could listen while reading science fiction, so the ceremony had lacked personal tone, and the solicitor had returned to his office shortly afterwards, saying that he would be in touch.

Paul had been given a cardboard box of Richard's ashes, and a shell with which he might scatter them over whatever hallowed place had a special significance for the deceased; the Director of the crematorium explained that the most usual hallowed place was the deceased's own back garden. Since the flat had no garden of its own, Paul had taken the box of ashes and the shell into the garden of Onslow Square, unlocking the gate with his own private key, once Richard's private key. He had scattered Richard's ashes into the wind, and the wind had blown nearly all of them back into his face and down the front of his cashmere jacket, which now hung, still ashy, in the wardrobe, since he did not like to have it cleaned.

It had all begun ten years earlier. It had begun with a funeral. Now the ten years were over, beginning and ending, his twentieth and his thirtieth year, both marked off with a death.


The graveyard in which Paul's mother was buried surrounded a small church. The church was in two pieces. The tower was Norman, and stood fifty feet away from the main part, which was not Norman. Paul's mother had belonged to the Chapel, but the Chapel had no graveyard, so this was the next best thing.

She had always liked the church as a building, but the ceremony and grandness she thought unnecessary. 'I like to talk to God as an equal, like a friend, not as someone to fear.' It is true that at the end Mrs Williams had not feared God or death, but met both with open arms, her only regret being that she could not take Paul with her. 'You'll be too good for this world, Paul. You'll be hurt, disappointed, and used.'

Paul looked away from the coffin to the Norman tower he had once climbed, persuaded by two boys he knew. They were to see something special. When they reached the top of the tower, five other boys, and a girl Paul knew called Jenny, had already gathered. The nine of them waited in silence for two more boys to arrive, and then the performance began.

Jenny had created a dance. Paul turned back to the coffin, and forced himself to concentrate on the body inside it. But it was Jenny's body he saw. When he lowered his head, and screwed up his eyes, Jenny began to unbutton her blouse. '*This good and faithful servant of the Lord ...*' The vicar sang an improvised prayer, making full use of his lower register, and Paul tried to remember all the films in which he had seen Flora Robson. Useless! Jenny held her blouse just off her shoulders, and rolled her head round and round. The boys began to clap in time. Paul thought it was a pity Jenny didn't have long hair.

'*Bounteous are Thy gifts, oh Lord ...*' His left foot had become icy cold, so he moved his toes up and down, making a squelching sound in time to the vicar's mooing. Back in the tower, Jenny had reached her underslip, and Paul desperately wanted to leave, but he knew that if he moved he would be laughed at. The two oldest boys, who were fourteen and attended the Secondary Modern School, were clapping wildly, trying to speed up the performance. Paul, thinking it would hide his fear, clapped wildly too.

But Jenny took her time. ('A *time to sow, a time to reap, a time to ...*' Cold water had seeped into Paul's shoes, and was making his toes too numb to twiddle.) Jenny had no breasts to speak of, but she stroked what she had, and allowed two of the boys to touch them. Paul's hands were sweating so much that he was forced to hide them between his thighs, and try to wipe them dry on his short trousers. Jenny came towards him, arms crossed across her chest, moving her shoulders round and round. He felt sick, faint; he was going to faint. She removed one arm. The boys were looking at him. He clapped even faster, but it was unconvincing. Jenny removed the other arm, and bent towards him. He had a headache, a bad one. She moved nearer. Nothing was in focus now, but the little mounds of flesh. They wobbled; she held her fingers underneath them, pushing them forward, and making them wobble. She bent down astride his right knee, and put one of the mounds to his lips. He didn't know what to do. The nipple touched his lips. It was hard and rubbery, like the valve of an inner-tube. He kissed it. 'Bite it.' He opened his mouth, and Jenny pushed in the nipple, and as much of the wobbly mound as she could muster. The other boys were delighted. Jenny's knee pushed against Paul's groin. He had to shift his position; it was too painful. 'Bill's got a big mouth. Give him a bite.' But Jenny moved on, and continued her dance.

First the back of her knickers was lowered slowly. Her bottom was pink with cold, but she was determined to make the performance last. Then, even more slowly, she rolled down the elastic at the front. The boys roared. Paul looked towards the stair of the tower, in case anyone had heard. Finally Jenny's dance became ungraceful, because the elastic round the legs of her knickers was too tight, and she was forced to turn her back on the boys, and bend down. This caused more excitement. The eldest boy, Roger, suggested that someone should fuck her.

'No, you.'

'Let's see you, Clarky.'

'Come on, then. Why don't you start? I'm not standing here all night, you know.' Two red lines encircled her thighs, where the elastic had gripped.

Roger, since it was his own suggestion, and no one else seemed keen to be the first, unzipped himself. Jenny was dancing again, trying to do the splits. ('Ashes to ashes, dust to dust ...') It was soon over. Jenny wiped the inside of her leg, and swore that he'd never even got it in. Roger said she was a lying cow. Another volunteer was called for, but none then could or would dare.

The wet clay fell on top of Mrs Williams in heavy chunks. Paul wished he could scatter loam, fine loam, but it was over. They were moving back to the gate. 'You'll be hurt, Paul ... Hurt, disappointed, and used.'

# A TICKET TO RIDE

The train was twenty minutes late, and Paul sat on a bench near the Gentlemen's Toilet on Platform Two. It was not a big station. The platforms were linked by a foot-bridge which he had crossed to sit here, having asked two separate people if this was the right side for London. *'Always double-check Paul. And don't ask the porters. They never know.'*

The wind made his eyes water. He thought it would be nice to pretend they were tears for his mother. He wished he could meet someone he knew. He would stand directly in the wind, blink, and say, 'She's dead', and they would think he cared. The more he thought about it, the more they felt like real tears, but if so, they were tears for himself, not his mother.

Why was it that he couldn't cry? He'd tried very hard. Crying was expected of him. It would have made Auntie Jean and Uncle Ted happy. 'Don't bottle up your feelings, Paul. Let them come out. It's all right to cry, you know,' Auntie Jean had said in her slightly reproachful voice. 'I'm all right, thank you.'

It was the least he could have done. He had blown his nose very hard, once, but they had not been looking. If anyone, he should have been the first to break down. No, Auntie Jean was bound to be the first, but he should have done something. He had, of course, tried to look upset, and when they had returned from the graveyard, he had gone to the bathroom, and splashed hot water round his eyes to make them red. Uncle Ted had met him on the stairs. 'The wind's given Paul a colour, Jean.' Why couldn't the wind have made him cry then, instead of now?

There he had stood above the grave, feeling cold. That was all he could feel. He didn't mind that she was dead. She was going somewhere better; she had been convinced of that. She hadn't liked this life very much. Paul wondered how she would get on in the next.

He was alone now. That must mean something, but what? There were advantages and disadvantages. He wouldn't have to come home every other weekend, or make up lies for not doing so. But then there wouldn't be the jam and cakes, and sometimes potted meat, to bring back to help with his budget. No ties or socks at Christmas – but then, trying to think what to buy *her* was a problem he had often prayed to lose. He would not miss her, because he did not like her, and he had been alone inside himself for as long as he could remember.

Paul went into the Gents for the second time, just in case the train had no corridor. He stood up against the white porcelain, and waited. Nothing happened. He turned away, and studied the wall opposite. In elaborate detail was a drawing of a woman being had from both front and rear.

The train was not full. Two other passengers got on with him. He chose an empty compartment, sat next to the window, folded his arms tight, and crossed his legs. Acid indigestion crept up into his chest and made him swallow hard to get rid of the taste. Paul noticed a briefcase on the luggage rack opposite. He would hand it in at the other end.

He had eaten too quickly because he was hungry. Even so, Auntie Jean had asked if he was slimming. 'Lots of girls would give anything for your hips, Paul. You want some meat on you. Here, have some more cucumber. I can open another tin of salmon, you know.'

'Expect he keeps slim, dodging all that traffic in London.'

Uncle Ted took his third piece of sponge cake. His buttocks overflowed the hard-backed chair. The effort for him to get in and out of an easy chair, he admitted with some pride, was not worth the rest.

A man came into the compartment, pulled down the brief-case, took a paperback from it, sat in the opposite corner, and began to read. Paul felt cheated; he had taken trouble to find an empty compartment.

'Aren't you going to stay until tomorrow night, and have your Sunday lunch with us? You don't see much of the country in London. You aren't working tomorrow, are you?' At this point, Paul had been forced into a bare-faced lie. 'Sometimes I do when they're busy. We take it in turns.' 'But they can't expect you to work the day after you put your mother away. Oh, Muriel!' Auntie Jean clutched at the furniture dramatically as she left the room. 'She's taken it very bad. They were so close, you know.' Uncle Ted bent another chocolate biscuit, to console himself. 'They're a bit damp, these. She will hide them under the sink.'

As sisters, Muriel and Jean had been anything but close. They had disagreed about everything it was possible to dispute. Deeply competitive, they had raced each other to get married, and having married, they raced to get all the rewards of marriage – a fridge, a car, a television set. Paul's mother was ahead. They had just paid the deposit, and moved into a new semi-detached house, when Paul's father had gone to see the doctor about chest pains. 'They shortened his life by telling him. He should never have known.' Six months from the day of the X-ray, he had died. It had been a relief all round. Paul had been nine years old. He remembered his father sitting in the garden in a new dressing-gown, crying, while passers-by stared at him, and Paul's mother repeated over and over, 'They shouldn't have told him. No one should know they have cancer, if they can't do anything.'

Paul swallowed again, and wished he had some Rennies. The compartment was nice and warm. The man sitting in the opposite corner reached up and switched off the light above his head. Nothing happened; the light stayed on. He removed the bulb with his handkerchief, and put it on the seat beside him. Sitting back in his seat, he smiled at Paul, pointed at the socket, then at the bulb, and said, 'Vandalism.' 'Yes,' said Paul weakly, and turned to look out of the window. *'Never talk to strange men, Paul.'* All he could see was the reflection of the strange man and the interior of the compartment. The man had closed his eyes. He had curly grey hair and a slightly suntanned face.

Auntie Jean had cried a great deal, and said that she had felt God's hand as it came down and lifted Muriel up to Him. And to think that Muriel would never sit in the garden again, or watch television. Paul had stood six feet above his mother, feeling his shoe let in water, and thinking of Jenny Crossley. He had been cold, with that hollow feeling in his stomach. Nothing mattered. He didn't care if he fell into the grave. He didn't care if his mother woke up, and turned out not to be dead after all. He didn't even care if they knew what he was thinking about, or the fact that he'd had an erection at his mother's funeral.

The ticket inspector opened the door of the compartment, and the man in the corner held up his ticket to be clipped. Then they both looked at Paul, who put his hand into the small top pocket of his jacket. The pocket was empty.

It was so silly. He had bought a ticket. How else would he have been allowed through the barrier? He could give the man his name and address.

If Paul had chosen to explain that he had just been home to bury his mother, the ticket inspector, who now stood leaning against the door with an expression of blatant mistrust, would have melted, and told him not to worry over such trifles as railway tickets. He might even have added the thought that all journeys have to end. But Paul did not plead that he was distracted with grief, partly because it was not true, but mainly because he did not think of it.

'The small top pocket of one's jacket, Paul, is the correct place for railway tickets, unless the weather is very hot, and one is forced to carry the jacket. If tickets are always kept in the same place, then one always knows where to look when one is challenged.'

'Challenged' was a word Paul's mother had used a great deal. She used it about the most ordinary everyday happenings. She had once been challenged in Woolworth's, and accused of stealing, and when the solicitor had refused to take F. W. Woolworth to court she had shouted louder than Paul knew she could, 'But my honesty was challenged.'

'Are you challenging my honesty?'

The ticket inspector stepped into the compartment, and slid the door closed behind him. 'What do you mean?'

There was no going back. Paul was desperate. He had searched the floor, the seat and all his pockets several times. The money in his pocket amounted to four shillings and sevenpence. A new ticket would cost more than that.

'Are you calling me a liar?'

'If the cap suits.'

'Fits,' said the man in the corner.

'What?'

'I think you meant "fits".' The grey-haired man leaned forward, his feet stretched out between Paul and the railway employee.

'All I want is a ticket. It's not a lot to ask. Can you produce one?'

Paul searched again in all his pockets, and scanned the floor.

'How much was your ticket?' The grey-haired man pointed the question at Paul, and everyone waited for an answer.

'Fourteen and threepence.'

'Would that be right?'

'Where did he get on?'

Paul said, 'Banbury.'

'Let's have a look.' The railway employee consulted a book, which he kept in a tobacco-pouch. While he was doing this, the grey-haired man looked at Paul, and Paul looked at the grey-haired man, who pointed to the empty light socket above his head, and the bulb he now concealed in the folds of his jacket.

'Fourteen shillings and threepence from Banbury to Paddington.'

'Well, that seems to indicate a degree of honesty.'

'Doesn't prove he's paid, though.'

'Never mind. Since we wish with all our hearts that British Rail could run at a profit, we'll pay you twice.' The grey-haired man gave the ticket inspector a pound note. 'I think I'll need a receipt if I'm going to get it off tax.'

All the time the ticket inspector was making out the white chit, he was watching Paul. Then he gave the chit to the grey-haired man, and left.

'I'm sorry I can't pay you back now. I don't seem to—'

'Please don't mention it.'

Paul who could think of nothing else to mention, concentrated on looking out of the window.

Richard leaned back, and wondered if he had ever appeared as pathetically helpless as the boy in the opposite corner.

You are not really looking out of the window, are you? You are seeing what I am seeing. You. You see your hands clasped and tucked between your knees. You see your blue barathea suit, and your black socks, which unfortunately have a red motif on their sides. Your shoes are clean, and your hands are small. Your face is waiting to be spoiled, perhaps longing for it. You've tried hard to keep your lips firm, but the roundness of the lower one, and the pinkness of them both, give signs of wanting to be touched. Now, do you feel your lips being touched? Is all your contact with the outside world imaginary. A red patch has started to spread behind your left ear because you know where my eyes are looking.

'Whereabouts in London do you live?' Now you are forced to look round.

'I have a flat in North London.'

'A flat?' Challenging the word, but not unkindly.

'It's more a bed-sitting-room really.' Even now, not 'bed-sitter'.

'North London is a large area.'

'Turnpike Lane.'

Back you go to the window, stiller than before, thinking of your bed-sitting-room, with its smell of gas, and the landlady who lets her cat 'go' in the bath on wet days, for fear of paw-marks on the vinyl linoleum. Or perhaps you share with lots of others, none of whom understand you, or knows your tastes.

'Do you live alone?'

'Yes.'

What a ridiculous question! First, because it stands out a mile, and secondly because I have no wish to know. Reflex action. I share a compartment with a young man, and within two minutes, I've found out that he lives alone in Tottenham. Why bother? I'm forty-five. I haven't been to bed with any-one for over a year, and what's more I don't want to.

So why do it?

Richard considered his own question. With eyes half-closed, he looked at Paul, while Paul looked out of the window. After searching his own mind, and analysing his motives, he discovered the answer with some satisfaction.

It was a game. A game because he was bored. He had finished *The Weapon-Makers of Isher*, and had given up on *The Illustrated Man*.

Richard closed his eyes. He never slept on trains. He had once slept past his stop, and missed an Extension Lecture on Scott. His students had waited ten minutes, and then organized a Brains Trust, which had proved so popular that he had been forced to chair it every Wednesday.

Yes, it was a game, an intellectual exercise to pass the time between High Wycombe and London.

But was that only self-deception? One way of finding out would be to follow the game to its logical conclusion. I am not interested in this young man, or indeed any other, except as someone with whom I share a compartment. Therefore I should be able to carry this preliminary approach all the way to a seduction in my imagination, and remain totally unexcited. If I have the merest flick of an erection before Hanger Lane, then the game is lost, I have been deceiving myself, and must return to prowling the streets.

Games have prizes. It's true that this young man does not know we are playing, but if I lose, he must have won. So what's the prize? For me, if I win, the satisfaction of proving myself right, and even if I lose, I have the pleasure of an erection. For him, nothing, win or lose. If he knew he was playing, he would assume victory anyway, so he needs nothing. Seems a bit one-sided, but never mind.

First Richard imagined himself undoing the boy's tie and the buttons on the front of the boy's shirt. He imagined sliding his hand inside the boy's shirt, across the boy's chest, and then resting it in the warmth of the boy's armpit, which, after a while, would become damp with sweat, and tingle. The hair there having been stroked.

'Do you find it warm in here?'

'No, not really,' replied the boy with damp and tingling armpits.

Next, the boy's highly polished shoes were untied and taken off, then the black and red socks pulled down, and slowly slipped over the boy's heel and toe. The short golden hairs on the boy's legs bristled with delight, as Richard's hands stroked the boy's calves up and down, and kissed the boy's knees, all the time allowing the boy's foot to rest on his own balls.

'Have you read much science fiction?'

'Not much. I find it hard to understand,' said the boy, who had stretched himself out along the seat, and was now releasing the top button of his trousers.

Paul closed his eyes. He had never been any good at conversation. The man would clearly like to talk, but the moment Paul had answered a question, his mind went blank. If it did not go blank, it went confused. Like the colours he saw after staring at a light too long, all dancing and darting about, colours like tadpoles, wriggling and fighting to get out. These colours he assumed to be thoughts, but the effort of trying to catch one made him sweat.

Paul examined the man by concentrating on his reflection in the window. It was obvious that he was unaware of being watched, for he continued to stare at Paul as though in a dream. From time to time, he would smile, and Paul wondered if this was because he was thinking of his own son.

Richard pulled gently at the boy's turn-ups, and the boy released each of his other fly buttons in turn, before they gave way. Pull, release; pull, release. The boy's underpants were quite ordinary, except that they had a slit at either side. (The makers had promised extra athletic activity.) Through the slits, Richard could see the boy's hip bones. Cupping his fingers slightly, he was able to reach inside the slits, and touch the edge of the boy's pubic hair, causing the boy's penis to dance up and down.

'What sort of books do you read?'

'True war stories. Anything with lots of action,' lied the boy with the dancing penis.

The boy rolled over on his stomach. Richard's hands remained inside the underpants, one hand clasping the boy's warm penis, the other shielding his vulnerable balls. The boy moaned quietly, as his underpants were pulled down gently, and put into Richard's pocket. This is the moment, Richard thought, that he will start to talk about his girl friend. The boy kept his legs together, until Richard began to stroke his buttocks with a circular movement, occasionally running a forefinger along the boy's cleft. Gradually the legs and buttocks parted, and the boy began to talk about his girl friend.

By this time the train was well past Hanger Lane. In another fifteen minutes, they would be in Paddington. Richard had won his game. At no time during his fantasy, had he come close to an erection. He decided to take the game a stage further.

Richard imagined the boy spread out along the seat, one side of his face pressed against the dirty plush. The train was jerking from side to side, and Richard was unzipping himself slowly.

He leaned forward, enjoying the moment before entry. The boy lay smiling, with his legs apart and his arse in the air, as though he were posing for his first snapshot, twenty years too late.

'Where do your parents live?'

'They're dead.'

Richard came out of his daydream, as Paul's head turned slowly from the window.

Paul was unable to see clearly for the tears that seemed reluctant to leave his eyes. They hung there like rain on a car window when the wipers don't work. The man was still staring. He seemed not to have heard. Paul repeated the words.

'They're dead.'

That did the trick. The collected tears poured down his face, clinging for a moment to his chin before dropping on to the lapels of his suit. The grey-haired man came and sat in the seat opposite Paul, and said he was sorry. Paul buried his head in his hands, and continued to sob. He was not crying for his parents: he was crying for himself, crying for his lack of confidence, his lack of knowledge, his lack of ambition, his lack of interest. And because he felt cold inside.

At Paddington, the man stayed with Paul in the compartment until Paul had stopped crying. He suggested that they should go to the station bar and both have a brandy, but Paul refused, saying that he should get home. When Paul felt sure he would cry no more, he and the man left the train, and the man asked again if Paul would like a drink, saying that he was certainly going to have one. Paul accepted.

The brandies were drunk in silence, Paul drinking his a little too quickly. Afterwards Paul thanked the man for the drink, excused himself, and went home to Turnpike Lane, full of brandy, but cold inside.

# MEETING FOR LUNCH

Richard went home to South Kensington. He had had a shock.

He was talking to himself; he knew it. Everyone who lives alone holds conversations with himself. Richard's conversations for the next few days were to be about guilt. Usually, when he felt guilty, he tracked down the source, and stopped it. Richard's way of stopping guilt was to justify the cause. With this done, he would be guiltless again, and ready for the next attack. Sometimes though, he did not rush to stop the flood of guilt. Sometimes he would bathe in it, wallow, and even swim.

He had never done it before. Never anything like it. He had lived alone for four years now, lived without sex for over a year without missing it. Was this a subconscious need becoming conscious? Like the way in which one can go without sugar in tea and coffee, once one has grown used to it, and then suddenly some day one gets off the Tube before one's stop, compelled to buy and eat two bars of sickly chocolate.

But there had been no erection, no thrill, no pleasure save that of proving oneself right. They had been simple pornographic fantasies on the four twenty-three from Birmingham, fantasies to pass the time, as one might fantasize about winning an award or being interviewed on T.V. Most fantasies use something tangible. The award would always be presented by the Queen, or the Prime Minister, or perhaps T. S. Eliot, and would always be for something one could do quite easily, if only the rest of the world were to behave well.

The tangible element this time had been the boy? But why sex, and why so extreme? Sadistic. No, the fantasies hadn't been that. Richard tried to think of a word that meant 'slightly sadistic', but there wasn't one, 'mildly sadistic', but there wasn't one. Anyway he hadn't been sadistic, slightly or mildly.

He hadn't been sadistic, but he felt guilty for it. Had living alone caused it? He was forty-five. There might be another twenty or thirty years of living alone. Were these years to be decorated with sadistic fantasies? He liked living alone, had grown used to it, enjoyed the freedom it gave him. He had friends. A club. He met people all day, almost every day. He looked forward to retiring into himself of an evening. Having to please no one.

He had once watched an old man walking down the street. The man looked like an undernourished owl, his tiny shoulders rounded, his enormous baggy trousers swinging. He wore spectacles like those one used to get on the National Health, and carried a very old cardboard filing-box under his arm. Richard had shouted, and run across the street, mistaking the man for his old tutor, but the man had turned out to be an eccentric, who slept in the Reference Library every day, after reading old copies of the *Church Times*. The cardboard file was full of abusive words he wanted the government to ban. Every night, he heard a new one, and those he didn't hear he searched for in the so-called 'educational' books. Some had been cut from newspapers, and some copied from fiction. He never damaged library property, for that would hamper his cause.

Richard was forty-five. The file under his own arm contained notes on the longer poems of Colley Cibber. No abusive words there. But there were twenty or thirty years to go.

A week after the episode on the train, Richard received a letter.

47, Turnpike Lane.
London N.22.

Dear Sir,

Find enclosed P.O. for Fourteen and threepence, which you lent to me on the train between Banbury and London. I was very grateful for it at the time, and hope it finds you well.

Yours faithfully,
Paul Williams.

P.S.   I got the address off your suitcase.

The following day (a Saturday), Richard collected a picnic lunch from Fortnum and Mason, and rode the Tube to Turnpike Lane. Clearly, if Paul worked in a shop, he would not be at home. But then Richard would find a park in which to eat his half of the lunch, and take home the other half, either to store in the refrigerator or to throw away.

Now the water in the bath was cold, but Paul must remain soaking in it for another ten minutes; that was the rule. In ten minutes, he must spend five minutes drying himself. Then it would be twelve forty-five.

He had woken at eight thirty, but he had stayed in bed until twelve. That was the rule.

Always, on days on which he did not work, Paul forced himself to remain in bed until mid-day. This did not make the day any shorter, but it prevented him from wandering around aimlessly, or gazing out of the window (window-gazing was against his rules). Often he had found himself standing in the middle of his room, unable to decide whether to move right or left, since there was no reason for doing either. Sitting still, he found hard.

Paul climbed out of the bath, and began to dry himself slowly. After five minutes, he stopped, and examined the underclothes he had slept in. Since he was not going out, he could wear them again. Paul put them on. A notice on the wall said to leave the bath as you found it. This was difficult for Paul, since he always found it dirty. Cleaning it out usually took up five or six minutes, but today Paul just pulled the plug out, and moved to the window.

At first he meant only to look at the weather, but a Number 43 bus had stopped at the traffic lights, its upper deck almost level with the bathroom window. He would never feel safe on top of a Number 43 again. The people he could see looked neither safe nor unsafe, nor did they see him. They sat close together, hands between their knees, holding books or bags, cleaning their nails with their tickets, waiting for the traffic lights to change and the bus to take them where they were going. Paul longed for one of them to look up and see him, but why should they? They had bought their tickets, and they knew where they were going.

He moved about the room, wearing an old mackintosh over his underclothes. Last night he had left his only pair of jeans in soapy water. Today they would be rinsed, and hung to dry in front of the gas-fire. The only other trousers Paul owned were those of his funeral suit, and they were at the cleaner's having clay removed from the turn-ups.

Ten minutes were spent rinsing the jeans in five lots of clean water. Then they were hung over the back of a chair, and old newspapers placed underneath its legs to catch drips. Paul dropped a shilling into the meter, and lit the gas. He didn't need trousers today. He wasn't going out. The bell above his door rang.

'I thought you might like some lunch.' Richard was holding a white carrier-bag. He and Paul stood facing each other on the doorstep. Paul played with the buttons on his mackintosh. Fortunately they were all done up.

'Would you like to come in?'

'Thanks for returning the fourteen and threepence.'

They stood in the hall for a full two minutes. To Paul it seemed longer. Then Richard asked if he might see the bed-sitting-room Paul had spoken of.

The steaming jeans were removed from in front of the gas-fire, and Richard sat on the floor saying that it was more like a picnic this way. Paul sat opposite him on the small brown hearth-rug, and Richard placed the ingredients of their picnic between them. He took a bottle of *blanc de blancs* and a cork-screw from the carrier-bag, and asked Paul to open the bottle. Meanwhile he sliced an avocado into two halves.

'I wonder if you have any olive oil.' Paul looked blank. Sometimes his mother had soaked her hair in olive oil before washing it, but Paul himself used a medicated cream shampoo.

Richard said, 'For a vinaigrette.'

'I've got some vinegar.'

'Ah!' Richard looked at the shelf above Paul's gas-ring, and found some Heinz Salad Cream. 'We'll use that. It might be rather jolly with avocado.'

The salad cream was not particularly jolly with avocado, but their picnic was jolly. Paul discovered that he liked dry white wine, and drank his half of the bottle. His worry at what they could talk about was soon forgotten, because Richard was asking so many questions. They went fully into the question of what Paul did for a living, which was to work 'casually' for an agency supplying temporary employees to temporary employers, so that he was engaged by the week, or by the day, or occasionally by the half-day. In the morning, he might be helping to re-decorate someone's flat, while the afternoon would be spent working as a male domestic. One week he would be serving in a shop somewhere, and the next pushing leaflets through all the letter-boxes in S.W.3. From time to time he would be asked to do office-work, but this never amounted to more than addressing envelopes or being a messenger.

Richard said, 'It doesn't sound as if you find it very interesting.'

'It's not.'

'But aren't you always meeting new people?'

'You don't meet many people when you're delivering circulars. And domestic work, they mostly leave you on your own. There was one Jewish lady in Willesden used to tidy up before I got there, and burst into tears when I tried to clean her silk sofa with a carpet-beater. She said she liked me because I wasn't a musician. She said all musicians were dreamers. I think she'd had bad experiences with them. The first domestic job I had, I got there an hour late, and broke a statue.'

Richard laughed, and what with the wine and having made someone laugh, Paul grew more relaxed, and the more relaxed he grew, the more he talked. He told Richard about his father, who had died of cancer when he was nine, and how his mother had gone to work as a typist (a job she hated), and how they had been forced to sell the house they had not yet paid for, and go to live on a council estate.

Richard tried to stand, and discovered that he had got cramp from sitting on the floor with his legs crossed, and supported himself with one hand on the mantel-piece. 'I think your fire's going out,' he said, and clearly the gas-pressure had dropped.

Paul had no more shillings, and Richard had none either. But there was another shilling-meter on the side of Paul's television, and the lock on it was broken. His usual shyness now quite driven out by wine and conversation, Paul opened the meter, and stole a shilling from it, explaining that he himself had broken the lock.

'There were these two men came round once a month to collect the shillings out of it. One was small and fat, and the other was tall and thin. They had a blue sugar-bag for the money. I used to make them tea, and they'd talk to me about my jobs and what there'd been on television – I watch it a lot, you see. When they'd installed the set, they'd said it wouldn't cost more than eight shillings a week, and anything over would be refunded when they collected the money, but what with them talking all the time and asking me questions, I forgot about the refund.'

Richard realized that the men had taken advantage of Paul's loneliness and need for conversation, and became very angry, but he did not allow it to show. 'So you broke the lock?'

'With a tin-opener. I was upset. It wasn't all that money being taken; it was being made a fool of. Only after I'd got it open, I couldn't lock it again.'

'So what did they do?'

'Nothing. They were so busy talking, they didn't notice. And they locked it when they left, but I must have damaged the mechanism, because it still opens.'

Richard was delighted by this, and asked where the loo was. Soon he could be heard peeing delightedly in the bathroom next door to Paul's bed-sitter. When he returned, he sat on the edge of Paul's bed instead of the hearth-rug.

They spoke about Paul's other jobs before coming to London. At fifteen, he had left the Secondary Modern School, and gone to work for a local builder. He was not strong, and therefore was only given light work to do. Then winter came, and the builder could employ him no longer, so he had cycled into Banbury and got a job as a shop-assistant, selling men's shirts and ties. For this he was paid very little. The manager told him that it was a gentle job for a man of the right temperament, but if he wished to make a fortune, he had better seek it elsewhere. Six months later, he had moved to a factory that made pork-pies, but after three days his mother had complained about the smell on his hands, so he had left, and come to London.

'Why?'

Paul considered. 'I don't know really.'

'To get away from home?' Richard had met, both as a university teacher and in private life, a great many young men and women who had felt a need to get away from home.

'I suppose. I went back for weekends.' ('*You'll be too good for this world, Paul. You'll be hurt, disappointed, and used.*')

'Yes, I know those weekends. Torture.'

In London, Paul had found a job in a Supermarket, filling shelves. Paul liked this job because it didn't require thought, and all the other shelf-fillers played games. These games were usually against the customers. One, he remembered, was the 'Deaf' game. All the shelf-fillers swore to feign deafness if spoken to by a customer, and if any shelf-filler were caught by one of the others replying to a customer's question he was forced to pay a fine from his wages. Paul frequently went home with only half of what he was due. When the management found out about these games they offered the shelf-fillers a Civility Bonus, which was promptly rechristened the Servility Bonus. A year ago, one of the more enterprising shelf-fillers had left to start the Agency for temporary work, taking with him six other shelf-fillers and the trainee manager.

At five thirty, Richard left, having made an appointment to meet Paul for lunch the following Tuesday.

At twelve thirty on Tuesday, they met at Speakers' Corner, and walked through Hyde Park to Bertorelli's in Queensway. Again Paul talked about his childhood, and Richard listened. After lunch, Richard went back to work, and Paul went home, since meeting Richard for lunch meant taking the whole day off work.

On Thursday evening, Richard phoned Paul to ask him about lunch on Saturday, and Paul promised to buy some olive oil. When Saturday arrived, Richard brought the lunch with him, and attempted to cook it on Paul's gas-ring.

After that, they settled into a routine. Tuesdays, lunch at Bertorelli's; Thursdays, lunch at Richard's flat; Saturdays, lunch in Paul's room. It was a courtship, but to what end?

The end was that the courtship should continue, and not end.

The routine lasted for ten weeks, until Richard suggested that Paul should take an extended holiday from the agency, and redecorate his flat at a wage of three pounds a day. Since Paul was finding it difficult to live on the seven pounds ten shillings he was paid by the agency for three days' work, it seemed an excellent idea.

When the entire flat had been painted, except for one room, Paul found that he was reluctant to go back to the agency. Richard then showed him that room, and asked him if he would like to live in it, at least until he found a job. The room had belonged to someone called Peter, who had lived with Richard for twelve years, before marrying a physiotherapist, and returning to the family sheep farm in New Zealand.

After Paul moved out of Turnpike Lane, and into Onslow Square, very little was said about work.

# MEN AT EASE

Sheepskin coats in autumn, beach sets in summer. Dukes, earls, pools winners, and young men who were being kept. Leslie was used to a variety of stock and customers. He removed an olive-green corduroy jacket from a model, and replaced it with a yachting blazer. Today he was in charge. He repositioned the model's arms, folding them on its chest to suggest the hornpipe.

The buyer had no flair. How could he, and live in Wembley Park? Once a week, on the buyer's day off, Leslie was in charge of the Men At Ease Department, it being the store's policy to try responsibility on their staff for size before they finally tailored it to fit for life.

Leslie's life had reached a turning-point this morning. New leaves must be turned over; today he was thirty-four. As always when he had the department to himself, he tidied, and dusted, and rearranged the stock. Even the shelves of sweaters he altered, so that the colours toned, and made an attractive backdrop for him to perform against. Today he was thirty-four. Today for the first time he realized that he looked every day of it. Today he was no longer pretty. He had served no one all morning, except two elderly lesbians, who had tried on all the men's jackets and hats, and bought nothing. He had turned the full-length mirror to the wall. He had lost too much hair for the careful arrangement of it not to show. He must brush it back, let the pink scalp show, and say, 'What the hell?' – but not yet. He must stop smoothing Nivea

Cream below and around his eyes, and accept the fact that all that disappointment is bound to show, but not yet.

A very beautiful young man came into the department, looked round, tried on a sheepskin coat, and bought it for a hundred and fifty pounds, using the credit card of a famous actor. Leslie had hoped, ever since he had arrived in London fourteen years ago to study drama, that somebody would keep him. He had never really hoped for fame. He knew his talent was too limited, and he hadn't the temperament for fame, but being kept he was ideally suited for. The longest he had ever managed it was for three months. Four times he had been kept for three months or thereabouts, and always it had ended in the same way. The person doing the keeping would say, 'You're wasted, Les. A clever boy like you should have a job,' and they would find him one, and then move to another capital city. Every Christmas he would get expensive Christmas cards from Paris, Rome, Madrid, Tokyo or the Bahamas.

He lunched on his own in the canteen, and looked out of the window down into Sloane Street. He lived in Fulham. It was a simple bed-sitter, but it was Fulham, and Fulham was In at the moment. 'Don't forget the rehearsal tonight.' A horribly spotty face reminded him that the store's Drama Club was doing *The River Line*, and he was playing the lead. He couldn't rehearse tonight, not on his birthday. He would get a bottle of wine on his way home, finish off the Tio Pepe he had left, watch television, and go to bed drunk. Giving up hope? People are doing it all the time in various degrees and for various reasons, but for how many does it happen so suddenly? One minute you're opening your eyes to the world, dragging yourself out of bed to greet it, and just as you're cleaning your teeth so as not to offend it, you look at yourself, and it's as if you had never looked before. Leslie remembered the face he had seen in the mirror, the eyes which had said 'Why bother?' and the muscles round the neck and mouth which ached from saying 'We aim to please.'

When Richard and Paul walked into the department, Leslie saw them at once, but they did not see him at first. Then suddenly Richard was being confronted by a face from his past. It wasn't even the face he recognized, but the worried expression round the eyes. Today the worry was accompanied by a knowing smile.

'How can I help you, sir?'

Richard couldn't find a name for this face. He remembered a party, and he remembered a bed. The grin on the face grew bigger, and showed some teeth, as though teeth were a clue.

'Hello. Yes, thank you. Please do.'

No, the teeth didn't help. 'How awful!' Richard thought. Had one really been to bed with so many people that they all became expressions? Now he wished he'd said they were just looking.

But he hadn't. 'We'd like some casual shirts and slacks, I think.'

'Yes, sir.' The smile knelt down to level itself with Richard's hips. 'Now, let's see. You'd be about ...' The tape was around his waist. 'Oh, yes; that's quite simple. Now the inside leg.'

'I think I should explain that we want them for this gentleman.'

'Oh, you mean you want them for this young man?' He doesn't remember, Leslie thought. But Leslie remembered. He mustered all the innocence he could. 'I'm so sorry. I didn't realize you were together.' He had talked to this man about life, and told him private things about himself that no one else knew. They had made love, and Leslie had given himself in a way he kept for very close friends. He must be invisible; it was the only explanation. How *could* the man not remember?

'What exactly had you in mind for the young gentleman?'

'I think the young gentleman may have something in mind himself. Let's ask him, shall we?'

Richard was angry, but to show it would be a point to the enemy. It was clear to him by now that the man expected to be recognized. But how to do it? One can't say, 'Excuse me, but did we ever sleep together?' in the middle of a rather grand Department Store, because they might not have. And to say, 'Don't I know you?' if they had made passionate love might be thought extremely forgetful. Yet he had forgotten.

'Well, sir? What had you in mind?' Leslie put down his tape measure dramatically, as if for a long wait. He was behaving badly. He knew it, but he couldn't stop. Meanwhile the young pasty-faced nit, who had stood silently gaping from one to the other up to now, began to speak, mumbling something about what would he suggest.

'Well, it's rather difficult, sir, since I don't know your tastes.'

Richard pointed in desperation to a crocheted shirt on a dummy. 'What about something like that?'

'Can I try it on?' Paul removed his jacket.

'Yes, of course. Why not? I think you'll find it much too large, though.'

'Haven't you got his size?'

'No, sir, not in that. As you see, it's really designed more for the maturer man.'

'You can't help us, then?' Richard said bitterly. 'You have nothing at all in our size?' He remembered now. The man was wiping his hands with a handkerchief. He had sat on the edge of Richard's bed, and explained how they embarrassed him, how at some interview, when he had come to sign his name on a contract, his sweat had made all the signatures run, and they had had to fetch another. The boy (as he had been then) had talked for hours about God and Life until Richard had been unable to keep awake any longer.

'Might I suggest that if Sir could give me an idea of colour, then I should know where to start looking.'

Simultaneously Paul and Richard said, 'Blue.'

'Well, we're unanimous on that anyway. Yes, blue is *always* popular.' That was his exit line, and with it he disappeared, but not for long. There was no time for them to leave.

'Here we are, then. Now there's lots of different shades of blue. There's more shades of blue than any other colour, I would think.' Leslie was getting into his stride now. Today he was thirty-four. Today was his. It was doing him good, and he could feel it. The actor in him had been thwarted for so long, ever since he had modelled for knitwear patterns seven years ago; the Drama Club's *River Line* couldn't be called demanding. Now it was a good Saturday night in rep, and he was playing the other woman. 'Has the young man got blue eyes? Because that would make things more difficult.' The question was thrown towards Richard, but there was no pause for a reply. A spring snapped in Leslie's head. For thirty-four years he had wound the spring up tight, and today, as if the guarantee had run out, it broke. Snap!

At first the machine carried on just as before, only more quickly. 'Perhaps Sir would like to try these on in the Fitting Room?' he said, throwing the clothes at Paul. 'Matching pair. Shirt and slacks in Marble Blue.' He moved upstage, and put his hand to the wall. 'Tapered shirt, as well as slacks.' He swished back a curtain. 'In there, and get your knickers down.'

Paul obeyed. Now Leslie sang *The Man That Got Away*, as he unpacked more and more boxes. 'There's just no let-up, the live-long night and day.' Blue sweaters, blue shirts, blue underwear and blue socks were hurled into the air. Placing a blue golfing-cap at a rakish angle on his head, he danced around the Men At Ease Department, grinning and winking. A crowd of shoppers gathered to watch.

Richard stood, fascinated. The man was clearly having a

nervous breakdown. Meanwhile Paul had changed into the slacks and shirt, which were much too tight. They were so tight, and revealed the cluster of his private parts in such detail, that he dared not come out from the privacy of the changing-room. Leslie had stopped hopping over the empty boxes and round the counters, and was trying the crocheted shirt on himself, while the crowd at the edge of the department grew larger. 'Eighteen guineas for this? I could knit it myself for four. The wind gets colder, and suddenly you're older; it's because of – Where is he? Where's Little Boy Blue?'

Quickly Richard moved towards the changing-room, but Leslie was there first. Paul tried to hold the curtain closed, and Richard and Leslie fought for it. Leslie won by a tear. 'What you hiding for? Show us your muscles.'

'I'm afraid it's too tight.'

'Nonsense. You look dishy. Doesn't he look dishy, sir?'

'Get changed, Paul.'

'You don't remember me, do you? That's the story of my life. Instantly forgettable.'

Paul hurried to squeeze himself out of the tight trousers, while Richard held up the torn curtain.

'No reason why you should remember me. After all, we only slept together once.'

A giggle went round the crowd. 'Could I speak to the Buyer?' Richard's hands began to sweat, as the boy's had done. He felt sick. He held the torn curtain between wet fingers, and his armpits itched.

'It's his day off. There's only me, I'm afraid, and I don't accept complaints. There's nothing wrong with my Department except the customers.' Leslie sat on the floor, surrounded by empty boxes, tears rolling down his face. 'We do our best, and we make a profit. Nobody should have a hundred and fifty pounds to spend on a coat.'

Paul was ready. As he and Richard left, two assistants, who had been standing on the side-lines watching, started to pick up the stock.

Quietly Leslie stood. Then he walked slowly to the Washroom to collect his coat. He would buy a bottle of wine, and finish the Tio Pepe.

# A SMELL OF LEMONS

Paul undressed himself slowly. The time was about three thirty in the afternoon. The sun, fighting to get past the roller blind, made everything in the bedroom a pale orange.

There were still things in the room which had belonged to Peter. The things were a bottle of hair tonic and an electric shaver.

Inspecting himself in the cheval glass, he found a small spot on his left shoulder, ready for squeezing. The tiny white head and trickle of watery blood were pressed into a clean handkerchief, and Monsieur Lanvin Cologne (a present from Richard) was dabbed on to cleanse the pore.

He wasn't nervous; that surprised him. This was his room now. He had spent the last two weeks redecorating it. He had passed hour upon hour, walking round and around Sanderson's, trying to choose a wallpaper. He had looked at William Morris prints, hand-painted Chinese papers, wallpapers that looked like planks of wood or blocks of marble. He had done thousands of sums, and worn himself out. Finally he had painted over the existing wallpaper with orange emulsion paint. The bed-cover was the colour of over-ripe red plums, and cost as much as the walls would have done if he had covered them with silk. The main object had been achieved, however. The room looked completely different. When he had first seen it, three walls had been covered with a paper which suggested carved oak panels, and the whole of the fourth wall had been painted in *trompe l'oeil* with a panora mic view of the Great Ballroom of the Palace of Versailles. Paul had imagined Peter sitting up in bed and conversing with the guests at the ball.

Richard had made no attempt to hide Peter's belongings. Why should he? They had moved his effects out together to make room for Paul's. They were not exorcizing a ghost. Peter's mark was still very strong on the flat. There was a large painting of him in Richard's study, which made him look as though he had smelt something sour.

They had given away his clothes to Oxfam, Richard making nervous jokes to the lady who came to collect them about earthquake victims being seen on television wearing Italian silk shirts. The woman had explained how the clothes would be displayed in an Oxfam shop either in Chelsea or Hampstead, and would most likely be bought by students who had come to the shop to look for cheap second-hand record-players.

Paul put on his dressing-gown, and waited.

Richard took off his jacket. It rattled. Three threepenny bits had fallen through the lining of the pocket, and were rolling around somewhere in the hem.

'This is ridiculous. I must either throw this out and buy a new jacket, or have all the pockets copper-proofed.'

He took off his trousers. They were their usual shapeless selves.

'Does one start dribbling at my age?' He was looking at the urine stain on the front of his underpants. He quickly decided that it was caused by not shaking himself after peeing. 'Everything gets rushed nowadays.'

He also observed how much he was talking to himself.

A long time ago, he had stopped considering his shape, and settled for watching his weight. Twelve stone was his limit. If he rose above that, he stopped eating bread and potatoes. He had never cared for them until he had tried to give them up. Twelve stone is not a lot for a man of six foot, but if half of it is below the midriff the total effect is not pleasing.

Richard suddenly realized that he would need a bath. Running into the bathroom, he caught the reflection of himself in the mirror, and laughed out loud at the sight of himself naked and in motion. He was nervous. That was the laugh of someone who was nervous. Paul would be nervous too, more nervous than himself. He must be very careful. Had he been wrong in suggesting it?

He had courted Paul, bought him expensive presents, had enjoyed buying them. But this had given Paul a sense of debt, and after the episode of 'Men At Ease', this had found expression in sullenness and always ordering the cheapest dish on the menu even if he was known to hate it. Then Paul had spent hours cleaning the car, his room, all the shoes he could find. His honour was at stake. Paul was an honourable young man. Richard wished he were less so. He had found Paul taking all the books from the bookshelves, and dusting them one by one. Richard had said simply, 'Shall we go to bed?' It was as simple as that, not difficult at all. Paul had looked up, and sneezed; he was allergic to dust. They had laughed, and Paul had said, 'I'll get washed.'

Sitting in the empty bath, Richard realized that it would not fill in time. It was sunken, and large enough for two people, which meant that it took twice as long to fill. Paul would be waiting. Richard soaped himself all over, lay down in three inches of water, and splashed it over him. He worked it out that if there were two bodies in his bath and both were pear-shaped and weighed twelve stone, they would have to lie end to end.

There are always things one forgets, stuffed away in cupboards or at the back of a wardrobe. As well as the hair tonic and electric shaver, Paul had found some photographs, holiday snaps, some in colour, but mostly black and white. One in colour showed Richard and Peter sitting at the table in a restaurant. They were laughing, Peter with his head back and his mouth open. The picture was slightly out of focus, and the colour not very good. It made their suntanned faces look as though they were wearing make-up. He left the photographs out on the dressing-table, to remind him to give them to Richard.

Richard knocked on Paul's door.

'Come in.'

He did. 'Sorry it took so long. I thought I'd better have a bath.' Richard was wearing his dressing-gown too.

They stood facing each other in the newly decorated room, not knowing what to do. 'Shall we sit?' Richard offered a hand, Paul took it, and they sat on the edge of the bed, side by side.

'I feel very nervous. How are you?' Richard said.

'All right.'

They remained still and silent for what seemed like hours. Richard had washed his hair. The dry bits stuck up in grey tufts, while the damp patches lay flat to his head.

'You've washed your hair.'

'Yes. It needs cutting.'

'Where do you go.'

'Gordon at the Green Park Hotel. I've been going there for years. Peter found him.'

'I found some photographs of Peter's under the newspaper in the bottom drawer. I'll give them you.'

'No, sit down. I'm not being very good at this. I'm sorry.'

Paul sat down on the bed again, and pulled the white towelling dressing-gown around himself. He wanted desperately to do something that would put Richard at his ease, but what? He had never been in this situation before, about to be made love to by a man. He had never even been about to be made love to by a woman. The only person who had made love to Paul was Paul. His experience was limited.

Richard plucked at the expensive bed-cover, and said, 'The room's looking nice and smart.'

Paul agreed. His back was beginning to ache. He lowered it on to the bed. Without hesitation, Richard leant over and kissed him. This was obviously what had been needed, the sign that they could continue.

The kisses were gentle, and they covered his face. At first he winced, as one does when licked by a dog. Paul closed his eyes, and Richard kissed the lids, gently moving his tongue from side to side across each one in turn. Paul rather liked this. He wrapped his arms round Richard, and held him close.

'Let me get rid of this.' Richard stood, and removed his dressing-gown. His round stomach stuck out, and his penis and balls hung loosely. He was not sexually aroused. Leaning over Paul, he said, 'Can we take this off?'

Paul allowed his white towelling dressing-gown to be taken off him, giving only a minimum of help. Then Richard lay beside him, and stroked his face, chest, arms and stomach. Smooth circling stroking movements, backwards and forwards, swishing and swaying, smoothly stroking in circles, round and round, up and down, always stopping at Paul's pubic hair. Paul shivered. *His* private parts were visibly aroused.

Richard moved down Paul's body, kissing it. First the nipples, winding his tongue round and round them as if to start them spinning. They tingled, and Paul, thinking he felt them harden, remembered his own mouth round Jenny Crossley's nipples, and their likeness to the valve of an inner tube. Richard was now circling Paul's navel. Finally he blew into it, and they both laughed. While they were laughing, he moved down lower, and started to lick Paul's balls. The hair on them prickled, and Paul was so excited that he couldn't keep still. Then Richard took Paul's penis between his fingers, and put it to his lips.

Richard's tongue and lips slid over the circumcision scar, and sucked with a steady pulsating rhythm. Paul felt relaxed, freed, as if he had taken some drug. The lower part of his body no longer belonged to him; he had given it up. Richard lifted Paul's buttocks, supported them, and pushed the remainder of him deep down into his throat, swallowing over and over again. Paul moaned. His insides were being drawn out slowly, and they were taking leave of every nerve as they went. Richard's saliva ran on to Paul's stomach. Paul was being eaten by some enormous giant, who had started at the most interesting bit, and he was going to die from an excess of pleasure. Suddenly he was running up a hill, and couldn't stop, faster, faster, nearly there, run, run, run, run, run –

Paul broke through the tape with a loud cry, and in a moment was standing on the highest of three plinths, shaking hands, and being told he could go to sleep.

Richard swallowed hard, and lowered the boy down on to the bed. Paul immediately rolled over on his stomach, and fell asleep. Richard stood up, and placed both dressing-growns over Paul. The boy was asleep. It didn't matter that he himself had not been sexually excited. He was emotionally excited by the responsibility.

Paul woke at about five p.m., because the two dressing-gowns had fallen on to the floor, and he was cold. He got off the bed, and started to dress. The photographs of Peter were still there, and the other things too. The hair tonic smelt of lemons. It was guaranteed to stimulate surface circulation of the scalp, and remove loose dandruff. He shook some on to his hand, like vinegar, and rubbed it vigorously into his head, as advised by the label.

'Are you awake?' Richard pushed the door open gently.

'Thought we'd want some tea. I've bought something sweet and sticky to go with it.' They moved into the living-room, where the tea was brewing.

'Did you have a good sleep?'

Paul nodded. The something sweet and sticky turned out to be two Danish pastries. Paul lifted one to his mouth. His hand smelt of lemons.

# TEN YEARS

For the next ten years, there was a sameness about Paul's days.

On the days when Richard was out, Paul would get up at about ten thirty, and for breakfast he would have two cups of coffee with half an orange or grapefruit or a piece of melon. During breakfast, he would flick through the *Daily Mail* and *The Times*, avoiding any political news. Then, from eleven fifteen until eleven forty-five, he would lie in the bath, thinking about the rest of the day. From eleven forty-five to mid-day, he would dry, dress and comb his hair. Then he would wash up the dishes from breakfast and dinner the night before, and prepare lunch, which might be soup, or a salad, or a boiled egg, which he would then eat while listening to the radio.

At two o'clock, he would go for a walk. Occasionally, during the walk, he might shop for a new shirt, or a pair of shoes, or a tie. Also he would often buy food for dinner, from a shopping list left for him by Richard. At four thirty, he would be back in the flat, to make and drink tea, and wash up after it, both the tea things and those left from lunch. At five he would have another bath, and change his clothes, in order to go out to the cinema, or theatre, or a party, or for dinner. Always at parties, Paul stood as close to Richard as possible, and smiled as much as he could. Even if Paul and Richard were dining at home, Paul would have a second bath anyway. Then he would watch television before dinner, while Richard cooked, and after dinner he would continue to watch television, but with the sound off, so that Richard could read science fiction.

On the days when Richard worked at home, Paul would get up at nine o'clock, and they would have breakfast and lunch together. The programme was otherwise much the same, except that sometimes in the afternoons they would visit an Art Gallery, or inspect some Historic Home. Once a year, they went abroad together for a holiday, always to somewhere different, always to somewhere warm.

During these years, Richard did not attempt to push Paul into any particular way of life. If Paul had expressed a strong wish either to be found a job or trained for one, Richard would have helped, but Paul never did express any wish of that sort. Richard did not intend to fall into the trap of 'making someone' of Paul. Paul must find his own interest. Richard had determined that, whatever else happened, he would not be responsible for changing Paul in any way. Consequently, after ten years of living together, Paul was essentially the same young man as he had met on the train from Banbury. But ten years older, of course.

# AN ADMINISTRATIVE ERROR

At approximately nine thirty on a Friday morning, Richard leaned across the breakfast table to pass Paul the butter, and dropped it. The sharp stab of pain he felt near his heart caused him to let go of the butter-dish and hiccup for breath. The attack lasted about two or three minutes; then he became unconscious, and fell on the floor. Paul struggled with Richard's body in an attempt to get it back to bed. Unable to move it more than a few feet, and unsure as to whether he should anyway, he left it where it was, and phoned the doctor.

The doctor examined Richard on the kitchen floor, and then phoned for an ambulance. When it arrived, he suggested that Paul should ride with them to the King Edward the Sevenths Hospital for Officers. Richard was carried down the three flights of stairs to the ambulance, wrapped in a blanket. He was already wearing his pyjamas, it being his habit to breakfast in them.

Richard was fifty-five. He had read recently in a Sunday paper how one could have a special medical check-up by computer, and had rung his doctor and B.U.P.A. to arrange one. It was to have been on the Wednesday of the week following his attack.

At the hospital, Paul waited outside Richard's private room, and the Irish Sister gave him tea. After an hour, he was told that there was no news. He was to go home, and they would telephone him if there were any change. Paul took a taxi back to the flat, and waited there.

At four in the afternoon, the doctor phoned to say that Richard was sitting up and asking for him. Richard came on the phone, and said that he was feeling weak but all right. He had apparently had a heart attack. He must stay in hospital for a while, and take life quietly when he came out. He asked for some things to be taken to the hospital, and Paul made a list.

Richard was finishing his evening meal of boiled chicken and mashed potatoes when Paul arrived. He looked pale and older. Paul found that he couldn't think of anything to say, so he asked, 'Shall I read to you?'

There wasn't anything to read from except the *Evening Standard* which Paul had brought with him, so he read from that. Richard explained that now he was not allowed to lift heavy weights, run, climb stairs quickly, or drink alcohol and other stimulants. He told Paul that he must think seriously about tying himself down to an invalid. He said that even if he followed the doctor's advice carefully, there was no guarantee that he would not have another attack, which could be fatal. Paul promised to think about it. The Irish Sister knocked on the door to say that tomorrow Paul could stay later, but that now Richard should try to get some sleep, it being his first day in hospital, and having had such a nasty shock and all. The Sister left, and Paul stood up in the small bare room, wondering if he should kiss Richard good night.

'I'll come in the morning, then. Bring your letters. Is there anything else you need?'

Richard said he didn't think there was, but that he would ring Paul in the morning from the phone by his bed. It could be Paul's alarm call. The only thing he knew about hospitals was that they woke you very early. Paul said he would go, then, and Richard held out his hand, and said he was sorry about this. Paul took it, and said so was he. They kissed. Paul said, 'I'll bring some books tomorrow,' and rode on the underground back to South Kensington.

The telephone rang, and Paul woke to answer it. Richard's voice said, 'They bring you tea at six here.' He sounded cheerful, and said he had slept well. He would need a new toothbrush, and would Paul not forget to bring *The Times* as well as the letters? The hospital had told him they'd had a run on *The Times* this morning.

At ten o'clock, Paul arrived at the hospital with *The Times*, a toothbrush, *The Collected Essays, Journalism and Letters* of *George Orwell* in four volumes, and some Cape grapes. He went straight up to Richard's room on the second floor. The door was slightly open, so he knocked. There was no reply. Assuming Richard to be asleep, he tiptoed in. A purple cloth with a cross on it, embroidered in gold, covered the bed. Beneath the purple cloth, he could see the outline of a body. Paul crossed to the wash-basin, and placed the toothbrush in a plastic cup. Then he heard someone running down the corridor. The Irish Sister rushed into the room, and said she was sorry. They should have told him. There must have been an administrative error. His friend had passed away just after seven, having had a very bad attack.

Paul stood and stared at the purple cloth covering Richard. The Sister held the door open, clearly wanting him to go. He gave her Richard's grapes, and left.

Later he found out that there had not been an administrative error. The hospital had notified Richard's only surviving relative, his sister in Rhodesia.

In the street, he wept. Without sound and almost without tears, Paul moved through the London streets on a sunny Saturday morning, realizing he had loved Richard, and breaking his heart.

The flat now seemed much bigger. He made himself a cup

of coffee, and moved through every room, looking for something. He couldn't remember what it was, but he knew that, if he kept looking, he would eventually recognize it.

Though Richard and Paul had slept in separate rooms, they had shared a large wardrobe in Richard's room. Paul placed his suitcase on Richard's bed, and started to pack. The flat was no longer his home; he must find somewhere else to live. He had too many clothes. Some of them had only been worn once. When the suitcase was full, he laid the remainder of his clothes round the bed in piles. He would have to go out and buy another suitcase, or borrow Richard's. Paul opened Richard's side of the wardrobe to get the case, saw Richard's five suits hanging in a row, and decided that packing could wait. Since he had nowhere to go, he would wait until they asked him to leave. He was not sure who 'they' were, but 'they' must be told. He supposed that he should also tell the people who delivered the milk and papers, the bank, Richard's solicitors, and the landlords of the flat. They would all know on Monday anyway. Richard had once joked that he would get a five-line paragraph in *The Times*' Obituary Column, so clearly *The Times* should be told.

Remembering that it was Saturday, he found the home number of Richard's solicitor, and rang him. He asked if it was all right for him to stay in the flat for a day or two, until he found somewhere else.

'I don't think there's any need for you to move out, old man. Look, why don't you come in and see me on Monday morning, say about eleven? I can't tell you how sorry I am. Only fifty-five! You must be feeling pretty shattered. Look, don't worry about the flat and everything; I'm sure you'll find it will work out all right. Yes, I'll ring *The Times*; we act for the editor. Eleven on Monday, then. You know where to come. It's in the book.'

Paul put down the receiver, and remembered what he had

been looking for earlier. It was a ring, given to him by Richard. He had not worn it much, for he considered his hands too thin to wear a ring without appearing camp. He found the ring, put it on, and went out to see a matinée of *Butch Cassidy and the Sundance Kid*.

Freebody and Lumprow had become Richard's solicitors the moment he had started to be successful. To be accepted by them was a sure sign that one was going to remain successful. Lumprow was no longer an active partner in the firm. He had made so much money by the time he was forty that he had left the office one day with a straw hat and *The Encyclopedia of Home Brewing* to follow in the footsteps of Gauguin. Every Christmas, he would send Freebody a hand-made Greetings Card from some island or other as an acknowledgement that he had received his share of the profits.

Paul was shown into Mr Freebody's office by a young woman who had severe Body Odour. He recognized it as not so much a body smell but that of woollen clothes which have been sweated into for too long without being washed or dry-cleaned. Mr Freebody steered a passage round the room to avoid the young woman, and offered Paul a drink. Since it was eleven in the morning, Paul declined. The young woman leant over Mr Freebody's desk, and asked if she could take this film contract to the typist, and Mr Freebody remained by his drinks cabinet until she had left.

'Did you notice anything odd about our Miss Kay, Paul? I may call you "Paul", may I? We did meet at a party once.' Paul nodded. 'Did you notice anything about her personal ... her person, I mean. Did you notice a certain ... well, shall we say ...?'

Paul checked that the door was closed before he spoke. 'You mean her body odour?'

'It is she, then?'

'I think her twin-set needs cleaning.' Paul was surprised at his own directness. It seemed a shame to him that people should go around, offending others with their smell, and never knowing it, simply because the others are too polite to follow the lead of the well-known advertisement for soap. This young woman presumably wondered why people constantly moved away from her, and had parents and friends who could have told her.

'I was beginning to think it was me.' Mr Freebody sat at his desk. 'I changed my shirt four times last week. I shall have to sack her. Pity! She only came to us a few weeks ago, having just broken off a long engagement. She's the best worker we have at the moment. Mind you, two other girls have left since she came. Now, down to work! I've been reading old Dicky's file. May I say how sorry I am?'

Mr Freebody began on a list of what Richard had owned – Building Society shares, Ordinary shares in various companies, several issues of Loan Stock, three insurance policies. Paul wanted to know what Loan Stock meant, but didn't ask. There were also the pictures in the flat – a Hockney, a small Chagall, a drawing by Henry Moore, and three pieces of sculpture by Elizabeth Frink. Mr Freebody had already made a rough estimate of Richard's assets. They added up to approximately £120,000, less death duties, and they were now Paul's assets. Even the lease of the flat, which had another four years to run, was his. Mr Freebody explained that Freebody and Lumprow would be only too pleased to continue acting for the estate, if Paul wished. Paul signed 'Paul Williams' on some papers, and was shown to the lift by Miss Kay. As they waited for the lift to arrive, he mouthed the words 'B. O.' several times, but couldn't make any sound come out.

Walking along New Bond Street into Old Bond Street, Paul looked into the expensive shop windows, and realized that he could buy what he wanted, but since he had never known what that was, he walked all the way back to his flat without buying anything.

# 'HOW ARE YOU THIS MORNING?'

Lying on the grass in Onslow Gardens, where he had scattered Richard's ashes, Paul thought about life. It had been an expression of Richard's: 'I'll go to the loo, and think about life,' or 'I'll sit down quietly with a sherry, and think about life.' It really meant that he was going to have a rest, but having a rest was a guilty thing to do, and thinking was always praised. Paul watched the gnats hover two inches above the blades of grass, then all settle at the same time to recharge their batteries. He thought about himself and life in general. He was thirty – almost – and starting to put on weight. The buttons on all his tight-fitting shirts were beginning to pop. He was eating for comfort, picking at cheese every time he felt depressed; he would buy in large quantities of Canadian Cheddar for fear of being caught with nothing to nibble. But fatness was not his real worry, since he had no one to stay slim for. His main problem was a heavy depression which he was unable to pull himself out of. He woke with it in the morning, and went to bed with it when the television closed down. He sat with it at lunch-time, and took it out to dinner with him in the evening.

The clock of the church in Onslow Gardens struck mid-day. Paul wondered what he would have for lunch. He could always go to a restaurant, and drink too much, and then sleep away most of the afternoon. But then if he did that, he would find it hard to sleep tonight.

The old white-haired gardener left by the gate which residents of the square have to lock behind them, and went home for his lunch. Paul watched people walk round the square. Everyone had an objective, even if it was only to walk the dog or buy a bottle of milk. Everyone seemed to have an immediate purpose, a reason for moving. On one of the benches sat a blind old lady with her companion. The companion read to her from *The Times*, and they talked of how the old lady would like her hair done. Their world was very small, but they didn't need a big one; they both had someone to talk to.

He lacked conversation; that was it. Before, he had thought of his loneliness as being caused by not knowing people, but it wasn't necessary to know people before talking to them. He had, of course, attempted 'Hello' and 'Good morning' to people like the man in the Off Licence, or the greengrocer, or the silly man at the corner shop who sang to himself, and sold everything in rhyming slang. But this was not conversation. He must put himself into closer contact with people. A job, of course, was the answer. But at thirty, with no training, no experience to speak of, and an Insurance Card full of stamps reading 'Non-Employed (Class 3)'? Only the night before, on television, they had said that the unemployment figures were the highest for ten years. Even if he could find a job, he would be taking it away from someone who needed it more.

On his way home, he passed the Park Leigh Hotel, and had an idea. After all, one way of meeting people is to stay in an hotel.

He had decided to take a taxi, though he could have walked it in three minutes, and was only carrying one medium-sized suitcase, almost empty. The taxi was to impress the hotel, but the fact that he was so close worried him. For a while, he walked in the opposite direction to the hotel, but this did not cure his fear that the taxi-driver would refuse to carry him such a short distance, so he took the tube for two stops to

Earls Court. This had two advantages. It was a reasonable distance from the hotel, and an area in which there are a lot of taxis.

The girl at the Reception Desk remembered his phone call, and hoped he would be comfortable. She handed him a card to fill up, and he did so. The porter, a small thin man with a badly fitting hair-piece, took his case and key, and they entered a rather old lift in which there was a mirror which reflected Paul from the chin downwards.

'Excuse me, sir. You didn't fill in the most important part. What is your home address?'

'A hundred and four, Onslow Square.'

'Onslow Square?'

'London, S.W.7.' Paul pretended to examine the interior of the lift, while the porter and the girl behind the desk stared at each other in amazement.

'You didn't have far to come, then, sir.' The mirror in the lift was at exactly the right height for the porter, and in it he studied Paul closely.

Paul said 'No,' and was shown into his room.

The room was small, but he had expected that. The bed was also small, and so was the rest of the furniture. A hard-backed chair, a small dressing-table containing a small shaving-mirror, a small basket-work chair with one small round cushion, had all been carefully arranged. Paul moved the basket-work chair, and replaced it with the dressing-table, but then he was unable to draw the curtains. When he pulled the bed three inches away from the wall, the flex of the bedside lamp, a Mateus Rosé bottle sprayed with gold paint, refused to reach the socket. The wardrobe, which was fitted, was too shallow to take his medium-sized suitcase, so he had to force it under the bed.

He had overlooked one thing already. Tipping. The porter, who had pulled a face at the receptionist, and stared at him in the lift, had taken on a completely different persona when showing him into the room. He had waddled his way around, drawing the curtains and smoothing the candlewick counter-pane, talking all the time. While Paul had groped in every one of his pockets for anything that felt like a coin, the man had been saying that, if there was anything at all Sir wanted, just to ask for Robert. That it was all first names here, and Robert was his. That they liked to keep it homely here, you see, not at all official, because of all their residents and regular guests. And would that be all, sir?

Paul handed the man a pound note, and the man had frozen into utter stillness. After a moment, he had moved to the door, and whispered, 'Thank you.' Paul had almost told the man that his name was Paul, and to call him by it, but he managed to bite it back.

Robert Crump, General Porter, was very surprised indeed at being given a pound note for having carried one suspiciously light suitcase twenty-seven yards. He knew it was twenty-seven yards, because he had measured it, just as he had measured out the distance from the lift to every room in the hotel. The hotel had thirty-five rooms. The distance from the front steps of the hotel (there were two) to the lift was eleven yards. He could add that to the distance between the lift and each room, and know exactly how far he had to walk with a suitcase of whatever weight.

He had done this arithmetic partly because his life was dull, and he needed something to occupy his mind, and partly because one never knew when information like that would be wanted. If, for instance, a murder were to be committed in the hotel, knowledge of that sort would be invaluable. So when he was given a pound as a tip by a young man who had booked into the hotel for a week, giving his address as somewhere just around the corner, a young man with a suitcase which couldn't have contained more than a change of underwear, he decided to investigate during his lunch hour.

Robert climbed the steps of 104 Onslow Square, and read the names on the door bells. Beside the top bell were the names 'R. EAST' and 'P. WILLIAMS'; Paul had not been able to bring himself to remove Richard's name. Near the bell was a grille for speaking into. The wrought-iron gate behind Robert clicked shut, and a woman who was clearly drunk weaved her way carefully up the four steps. It was ten past mid-day. The woman look him up and down as she rummaged in her bag for her key.

'Are you from Harrod's?'

Robert replied that he was not.

'They haven't sent the sausages.'

Robert said he was sorry. The woman had been poking the key towards the door, but was unable to find a suitable hole in which to turn it. Robert thought he might help, and said so.

'No, thank you. I live here.' Leaning over and spraying him with gin fumes, she chose one of the bells, and pressed it with the palm of her hand. Back came a distorted reply.

'Jim? Open this bloody door. The key won't fit.'

There was a buzzing sound, the door opened, and the woman stumbled in. Before the door snapped closed, Robert held it open for a moment. It was very tempting. No self-respecting sleuth would pass up the chance to discover more. He could always pretend that he was delivering sausages from Harrod's to the wrong door. Reluctantly he decided against it, and walked back to the hotel, slowly revolving a bottle of Friar's Balsam in his pocket, and working out subtle questions to put to the suspect.


'How are you this morning?' Every morning Paul asked and was asked this question several times. Everyone in the hotel, it seemed to him, had a morbid curiosity about everyone else's health. It was not until he had been there almost a week that Miss Cartwright explained to him why.

'All of us here are going to die. Well, everyone has to do that, but we are likely to die soon, and we don't want to be alone when we do it, as badgers are supposed to prefer. Most guests in this hotel were living on their own, many quite near here. But we all had the same fear. Falling down and dying slowly, or not being found until we were decomposing. I don't see why that should bother us when we're dead, but it does.'

Death was known to be Miss Cartwright's favourite topic, and all the other guests avoided her for it. Because of this, she sought out Paul. Every morning he would ask her how she was, and every morning she would have a different symptom. She had studied *The Home Manual of Disease and Its Cure* from cover to cover several times, and had, she bragged, diagnosed in herself every ailment listed in the book's five hundred and seventy-three pages, barring miscarriage.

This morning she was on her way back to the shop which had sold her 'this'. Miss Cartwright pushed a carton of soapflakes under Paul's nose, causing him to sneeze. She had developed a rash, she said, after washing out what she described as her delicate bits. 'I always rinse them through before breakfast. Then the rest of the day is my own.' As she said this, her delight at having found a project for the day, a visit to the grocer's to talk about enzymes, faded for a moment, and Paul knew that 'the rest of the day my own' meant just that for all the guests of the Park Leigh Hotel, including him. There had been two Americans who had come to find a 'a typical English hotel', but they had moved out after one day.

Miss Cartwright and Paul shared a table in the Dining-Room. They went in together for breakfast, and Miss Cartwright placed her box of rash-giving soapflakes underneath her chair.

'What's that?'

'What?'

'Under Miss Cartwright's chair.'

'Her feet, I suppose.'

'Don't be silly. Look round, and try not to be conspicuous.'

'Dammit, it's a box.'

'Of what?'

'I didn't see. Do you want me to look round again?'

'Finish your grapefruit first.'

Miss Cartwright betrayed definite signs of glory.

On Friday, Paul booked into the Park Leigh Hotel for another week. He had not given it a fair trial, he told himself, but the main reason was that he didn't want to go back to the empty flat. He made up his mind to spend the next week looking for an hotel where he might meet someone under the age of sixty. Here, it was true, he had talked to people, but mostly he had been talked at.

After the funny looks he had been given by the receptionist and Robert, the porter, on his arrival, he had thought some explanation was necessary. So, after unpacking, he had gone down to the Desk and told the girl that he had moved out of his flat for a few days because workmen were rebuilding the back wall of the house, and therefore he had no kitchen or bathroom to speak of. He told her that the workmen had promised to be finished by the end of the week. Paul was not sure why he had added the last bit, except that it seemed to round off the story. Having given the workmen a finishing date, he now had to explain to the girl at the desk that they had run into a snag, and would be another week. The girl showed no interest whatsoever, except to say that nobody worked hard nowadays, and returned to her copy of *Private Eye*.

From time to time, Paul had the feeling that he was being

followed, and once Robert had appeared as if from nowhere, and asked him if he reckoned much to Fidel Castro. Another time, Robert had stopped Paul on the stairs and wished to know if he had ever seen Roumania in the Spring. Paul had replied 'No' to both these questions, but it hadn't stopped the porter's curiosity. A day later, after reading a newspaper story about the Mafia, he had asked if Paul had any Sicilian blood in his veins. Paul had replied quickly, wishing to end the interview, that the nearest he had ever got to Sicily was Southend.

Immediately, and with shame, he had remembered his trips abroad with Richard. That, at least, had happened. Away from the flat, he had thought less and less often of Richard. Instead he had talked to people, had conversations, even if they were a little one-sided. Mr Lodge had talked to him on the subject of Landscape Gardening. The Claradon sisters had spoken of their mother and the Bloomsbury Group. Then, of course, there was always Miss Cartwright, ready at meal times with a medical reason for not eating this or that. He had tried once to miss dinner in the hotel, and eat it out, but her reproach when next they met had been too great for Paul. So he presented himself at every meal, and widened his knowledge of medicine. She declared that the fact that he had been seen smoking kept her awake at nights. Paul had taken to smoking about five cigarettes a day, but never after meals with Miss Cartwright.

Robert bought a Russian Phrasebook from W. H. Smith's bookstall at the Cromwell Road Air Terminal, and from time to time greeted Paul with a phrase from it. He was convinced that when Paul heard his native tongue spoken there would be an expression on his face which would reveal all. The meaning of the phrase was unimportant, so Robert studied those he considered the easiest to pronounce.

When Russian failed to raise the desired response from Paul, Robert moved on to Cuban (which he knew to be Spanish with an American accent), and then to Chinese. W. H. Smith's explained to him with patience that they were not issued with a different phrasebook for the Red Chinese, but that the cover of the book was red, and they supposed that meant something.

Chinese proved very difficult, and by this time Robert was no longer convinced that Paul was a spy, or even a Corsican gangster, but he had found a project, and it was far too interesting to throw away. He would still find out all he could about the suspect, to whom he would now refer as 'the subject'.

It was unfortunate for both Paul and Robert that the first should discover the second stealing from his room. If Paul had not returned to his room to get the present he had bought Miss Cartwright for her birthday, no one would have lost by the attempted theft. Paul was not even sure that it *was* an attempted theft. He knew that one can't be charged with shoplifting until one has left the shop. But Robert had not left. He was still standing in the middle of Paul's room, flicking through the pages of Paul's diary. Paul's best jacket and its contents were splayed out over the bed.

Paul asked Robert what he was doing, and Robert's entire life passed before him. Suddenly what he was doing became the most important question in the world, and he couldn't answer it. He knew what he was. He was a porter. He was forty. He was a small thin man, who had lost two-thirds of his hair by the time he was twenty-nine. He was unmarried, but certainly not queer. He knew he was not that, because they had tried it on him in the Army, but he couldn't take to it. He lived alone in a room in West Kensington. He was a porter. But what was he actually doing? Going through somebody else's pockets.

He had never done it before, he swore. It had been a compulsion; he knew that. But why? Robert explained to Paul about his interest in detective work, and how he had thought it odd, Paul's arriving from around the corner with a light suitcase. He described the visit to Paul's address, and his meeting with the drunken lady. He spoke to him of the dullness of being a porter, and of the things that play around in one's mind when one has very little to do. Paul sat on his bed among his belongings, and listened, while Robert sat on the edge of the wicker chair, and talked.

He had stayed in the Army until he was thirty. Then the Army had given him three days to decide what job he wanted to train for. He hadn't known. He couldn't train to be a detective, even a private one, because he had no G.C.E., and anyway his height (five feet, five inches) was against him. After three days, during which he tried to get used to civilian life and decide on a job, the Army wished him luck, and thanked him for his twelve years' service in their Stores.

For two months, he had searched for an interesting job. After that he began to look for any job. When he had been out of work four months, people began to think he didn't really want work. 'So after a while, I went to this Agency. They suggested I invest in a hair-piece. I still had a bit of money left from what I'd saved in the Army, so I got a good one.' He patted it with his fingers. 'You wouldn't think so now, would you? The day I had the last fitting for it, I came straight on to an interview here, wearing it, and got the job. I've been here ever since.'

Paul explained that he really must go down to Miss Cartwright's birthday tea in the dining-room. No, he would not tell the Manager what had happened, on condition that they finished their discussion when Robert came off duty. Robert agreed enthusiastically. Paul told him that he mustn't be caught stealing again, because if he lost this job he would find it very hard to find another, even with a toupée. The unemployment figures were the highest for ten years. He was sorry that there was nothing of interest in the diary, but he only kept it in case he had any dates to remember.

When they met again, it was in the nearest Wimpy Bar. Paul treated himself to an Eggburger, and Robert to a Brunch-burger Grill. This was Paul's second meal within an hour, the first having been served with Miss Cartwright. They ate their meal in silence, but when the coffee came Robert placed his napkin in his saucer to catch the drips, and said 'It's the job that's really to blame. No advancement. The best thing you can hope for in this job is to rise to be Head Porter, but Park Leigh don't have a Head Porter. I'm their one and only.' The large hotels in London, he said, didn't want middle-aged porters, but attractive with-it ones.

'Some of them are allowed to wear their hair long, you know.' Robert patted his hair-piece. The reason it didn't fit him any more was simple. It had shrunk. 'I washed it very care-fully in luke-warm water with Drene Shampoo, and dried it in front of the gas fire. When I went to put it on, it looked like a Brillo Pad, all knotted up.'

He had taken it back to the shop. 'They said they'd told me I must bring it in once a month for a thirty-shilling dry-clean. If they did tell me that, I didn't hear them, but then I was very nervous about wearing it in the street, and the interview for this job. Now they said it would cost fifteen to twenty guineas before they dare touch it. They were very lah-di-dah in there. Well, they're only there to make money out of you, aren't they?

'I'd had it on for two years, and it'd got dirty; it needed more than a dry-clean, to my mind. Some of the knots where they fix the hair to the mat thing had come loose, so that the wig was getting bald, as well as me. It sounds funny now, but it wasn't then. Anyway, when I told them this, they said it would cost a hundred pounds for a new one. One of them saw the look on my face, and he took the wig away, and tried to reshape it a bit, and then he came back and charged me a pound. I haven't washed it since.

'It's very blond, isn't it? It gets blonder and blonder every summer. When your hair gets bleached by the sun, you can have it cut, can't you, but you can't do that with a hair-piece. I tried to dye it with a dye from Woolworth's, stroking the dye in gently with a toothbrush, but it went a sort of apricot colour.

'I know it looks a mess. I only wear it because I've got used to having it there.'

Lunches at the Wimpy Bar became the regular thing. Paul neglected Miss Cartwright and the other guests, and concentrated on Robert. They would spend an hour together at lunch time, and another hour over a drink in the local of an evening. Robert had been taking his half pint of draught Guinness at the same bar ever since he had started work at the Park Leigh. Paul drank a half of bitter. When introduced, the landlord told Paul that Robert was his best and most perfect customer. 'Always quiet, never in trouble, and always knows when he's had enough.' This was a joke, since Robert had just explained that he never under any circumstances drank more than one half pint.

At the end of the second week, Paul moved out of the hotel. He now had an interest and a friend. They continued to meet in the Wimpy Bar at lunch time, and the pub at night. They met every day; weekends were the same, since in Robert's job there were no weekends to speak of. They talked a great deal, because talking was not difficult. Paul remembered Richard's saying, 'Ask them about themselves', and on this subject Robert was very voluble.

He talked of his life as a boy soldier, of his sister who was epileptic, of the village in County Durham where he was born, and from which he escaped to the freedom of the Army instead of going down the mines. Of his father, who drank and was afraid of cockroaches, and his mother who ran away to Liverpool to become a tart. Occasionally he would stop for breath, or to fill his mouth with fried egg, and Paul would get in something he had been saving up about *his* mother, or *his* schooldays. He never spoke to Robert of Richard, or his present situation, though he did expect Robert to ask him about it, being an amateur detective.

Meeting twice a day, every day of the week, continued for another three weeks. Then, one day, Paul decided to cook lunch for Robert. They had both been getting bored with Brunchburger Grills and Frankfurter Salads. Neither of them had dared to suggest moving to another place for lunch, in case it did something to the ease of their conversation. Finally, when Paul had reached the stage of ordering something and then leaving it, and Robert had got to eating both meals because he couldn't bear the waste, Paul said, 'Will you come to the flat tomorrow for lunch? You know where it is.'

He had saved up the invitation until just before they parted, so that there could be no questions about the flat and his situation. At first he thought Robert was going to say No. He looked exactly as he had when Paul had tipped him the pound note. His eyebrows lifted half an inch, pushing the Brillo Pad of hair with them.

'Number a hundred and four, is it?'

'Yes. Onslow Square.'

Paul left Robert standing on the corner of the street, and wondered whether it was safe to let him cross the road on his own; he looked so stunned.


'The workmen have finished the back wall, then?'

Paul had to think for a moment before he knew what Robert was talking about. 'Yes.'

Robert examined the paintwork closely. 'It doesn't look very new.'

'That was the agreement under which they did it.'

'How's that?'

'Well, they had to put everything back exactly as they found it.' Paul was surprised at his own quickness.

'That smells good. What is it?'

'Filet de Boeuf Villefranche. It's just steak really.'

He had intended to stick to something safe, and grill some steak. Having made this decision, he realized that he didn't know how long to grill it for, or if you added anything to it. None of the five cookery books left by Richard gave a recipe for grilling steak, so he had chosen this, since it included steak. The steak was fried gently in butter, to which white wine and tarragon were later added, and garnished with chopped hard-boiled egg. Paul thought it delicious, but Robert ate very little. He kept remarking how good it was, and scraping the sauce off the meat. He couldn't drink the wine Paul had uncorked because 'Wine gives me acid', and Paul had not thought to buy a bottle of Guinness.

Paul enjoyed the meal, and talked far more than usual, partly because Robert talked far less, and partly because he was drinking too much. Robert had to get back to the hotel, and couldn't stay for coffee. Paul did the washing-up slowly, and then went to bed to sleep off the wine.

At four, he got out of bed, and went into the bathroom to wash his face in cold water. He stood as still as he could in front of the mirror for a long time, in order to give himself a fair appraisal. He discovered four more grey hairs, and realized that the corners of his eyes and mouth turned down, not just for this moment, but permanently. Even when he smiled, the edges of his face betrayed the disappointment he felt. Like the man in the Men At Ease Department, dancing around with an expression on his face that said 'Is this all? Can I expect no more?' Leaning closer to the mirror, he saw the small red blotches of broken veins high on his cheekbone. These, he guessed, were caused by too much drinking. His lips were pressed tightly together, defending each other from attack. He placed them against the mirror, and longed for an attack, any kind of attack. He wanted someone to touch him, stroke him, use him if necessary, but make contact. Twice recently he had travelled in the Tube at rush hour, simply in order to press himself against somebody. Leaning over the wash-basin, his head pressed hard against the glass, Paul asked for help.

'Please, help me. Someone help me. Talk to me. Touch me. Kiss me. Stop me from going mad at thirty. I'm only thirty. It's such a waste.'

Crying had made his face red. He washed it again in cold water, and combed his hair forward. It was much finer than it used to be, and there was a greasy patch on the left side of his crown. The ageing process had started, and he could expect another forty years of it. Paul let his pyjamas fall to the floor, and walked about the flat looking for his clothes, with a feeling of self-disgust. Could he expect another forty years of that?

Robert and Paul met that evening in the same bar, but conversation was difficult. Paul realized that he had made a mistake by drinking and talking too much at lunch, and was determined that tonight Robert should run the conversation as usual. But Robert sat as if in a stupor. He left before the hour was up, saying that he was sorry he hadn't been much company, but that he'd had wind all day. He said 'all day', and that would have accounted for his behaviour at lunch, but Paul knew that he meant 'all afternoon', because Paul himself got wind when he ate in a tense situation.

Paul drank another half pint of bitter slowly, and went

home to bed. Next day, as they ate their Wimpy Bar lunch, Robert showed no signs of wind, for he ate quickly and with energy, but the conversation was left to Paul, and Paul ran out of it quite soon.

Two nights later, when matters were no better, Paul decided to try to cook lunch again, on the grounds that they would be more relaxed the second time.

'Tell me if you think it's not a good idea. I'll get you some Guinness. Is there anything you don't eat? I'll keep it plain. We don't want anything fancy, do we?'

'Beetroot's the only thing I never touch. Don't know why. I've never tried it, but I don't want to.'

'We could have lamb, with new potatoes. Or pork. Which do you prefer?'

'Anything'll do for me. I'm not fussy.'


Paul got up at seven thirty, and spent the entire morning cooking. This amount of time was not necessary for roast lamb and new potatoes, but he was nervous, more nervous than he had been the first time. He bought six bottles of Guinness, and kept three of them in the fridge, and three out of it. He would drink Guinness too. Since he disliked its taste, that would stop him from drinking too much.

At one o'clock, the delicious smell of roast lamb filled the flat. The joint of meat was far too big for two people; he would be eating it cold for weeks. At one fifteen, Paul turned the oven down, assuming that someone had booked into the hotel just as Robert was about to leave.

At one thirty, he poured himself a weak whisky and soda to stop himself shaking, and at two o'clock he took the dry meat out of the oven and slowly wrapped it in aluminium foil.

Robert was not in the pub that evening, nor at the Wimpy

Bar the next day. After toying with an Eggburger Grill, Paul walked towards the Park Leigh, intending to ask if Robert were ill, but when he got close to the hotel he saw Robert standing outside on the steps. Paul dodged into a doorway. Then he went for a walk in Kensington Gardens.

For the next three weeks, Paul slept until mid-day, then got up and had lunch, and went for a walk in the park, or tried to read. But he always lost interest in a book by page ten, unless it was by Orwell. Richard had introduced him to the novels of George Orwell, Evelyn Waugh and Graham Greene, but Orwell was the only one Paul went back to, and those three writers were the only ones he knew. There were many other books in the flat, and he did try them, but always by page ten, he found that his own thoughts pulled him away. Often his own thoughts would only toy with him for a few moments, and then give up, but the effort involved in going back to the book, and trying to remember what he had read so far, was too much. He could never pick up a book, and select a page at random – perhaps page ten – asking 'What have you to offer?' This would be to use a book, and to Paul books used you.

He had taken to visiting three or four pubs a night. He liked the noise. He would sit in a corner, never at the bar, and hope that someone would speak to him. Occasionally someone did, but Paul was incapable of sustaining the conversation. After asking the person about himself, he would lose concentration, and forget what the man had replied, so that he was afraid to ask more in case he repeated himself.

One night Paul walked into a pub called 'The Shoulder of Mutton', and found Robert sitting in the corner with half a pint of Guinness in front of him. Paul collected his half of bitter from the bar. At first he thought Robert was going to get up and leave while he was doing this, but Robert's glass was still two-thirds full. This was Paul's fourth pub this evening, and he was already feeling rather drunk. He sat beside Robert, who gave a little nod, without looking up. Neither of them spoke for a long time. Finally Robert burped, and Paul told him he shouldn't drink when he was tense.

'I suppose I owe you an apology.' Robert still hadn't looked at Paul.

'There's no need. I thought you were ill; that's all.'

'Well, I was a bit depressed, but I can't put the blame onto that. No, I didn't come, because – well, it's funny, isn't it? We'd talked a lot, but I couldn't think of anything more to say to you. I must have used it all up, I suppose. In the Army, you don't have to think about conversation; it's just there. You can sit around for hours, talking about nothing, passing the time away.' Robert took a small sip of his drink, and removed the line of froth from above his upper lip neatly. 'What I'm trying to get round to is that the reason I didn't turn up for that lunch was because it wouldn't have worked out.'

'What wouldn't?' Paul was feeling ill. He could smell the beer as he lifted it to his lips, and it smelled of old soap. Perhaps the glass had been cleaned with a dirty rag. The floor pulsated up and down slowly, but no one seemed to mind this except him. Meanwhile Robert chatted on.

'Anyone can make money nowadays, provided you're young, and your hair's your own. Look at all these pop stars and models; their managers are no older than they are. You didn't know I could whistle, did you? I'm not allowed to in the hotel, of course.'

'Why not?' He wanted to lie down, but there wasn't room, and if he did, he knew it would make him sick.

'Because of the old people. Oh, it's not that they don't like it; they do. But it starts too many of them crying.'

'I meant, "What wouldn't have worked out?" and "Why not?"' The noise in the bar was making it difficult for him to hear Robert, so he leaned forward. This caused Robert to lean back, and talk even more quietly.

'What I mean is, we don't really have much in common to talk about, do we? I mean, I didn't realize you had as much money as all that.'

'Do you know how I got it?' Robert shook his head, and took a larger sip of Guinness. 'What do you know about me?'

'Not very much, I suppose.'

'You mean you don't know why I live alone in an expensive flat?'

Robert patted his Brillo Pad of hair, and glanced round the Public Bar guiltily because Paul had lifted his voice. Paul stood, to illustrate his feigned surprise. 'I thought you were a detective. You sat there talking about yourself for hours, but you never listened to me. If you'd listened, you'd have wanted to know how I got the money.'

Everyone in the Public Bar was pretending not to hear what Paul was now shouting hysterically.

Robert said, 'Why don't you sit down, and have another quiet drink?' He had risen to go to the bar, but Paul blocked his way. Paul felt the room start to turn slowly. Soon he would fall, or be sick, or both. The half bottle of wine he had drunk instead of dinner, and the five or six whiskies since, plus a sherry before the wine, and this soapy half of bitter now, were all conspiring to stop him saying what he wanted to say, what he needed to get out of his system. He held on tightly to the high-backed bench, and tried to ignore the faces that whirled and danced round him.

They were children's faces, and this was a game. He was in the middle, because it was his turn to choose a wife. Paul tried hard to concentrate, but the faces moved faster, some chanting a rhyme that he couldn't remember, others screaming at him to choose them. 'Me, me, me! Choose me! Quick!' Their throats were tight, and their faces red.

'Quick, quick, quick!
Who you going to pick?'

Robert sat down again, and concentrated on the froth which the makers of Guinness are so proud of. He was glad that he had always stuck to half a pint. Now he would have to find another pub in which to drink it.

Paul was by now feeling so ill that he had lost the urge to shout his secret to the world, and anyway there was only one person he really wished to tell. He sank on to the bench beside Robert, and took his hand. It was dry, unlike his own. And it was even smaller. Robert shuddered visibly, and shifted a little so as to cut off any association with this boy, who had been crying and shouting, and was now holding his hand. Paul held the hand tighter, and leaned against Robert's shoulder. The hair on the back of Robert's neck was his own; it was black and curly, and three or four of the same hairs curled round the lobe of his very red ear. Paul wanted to tear off the Brillo Pad of ludicrously blond hair, and burn it in the large glass ash-tray on the table in front of them.

'I was kept.'

He had whispered it into the round red microphone that looked like an ear. The children's game stopped, as if caught forever in a snapshot. He had chosen who his bride was to be. Now it was his turn to join the circle. But the circle wouldn't start. They hadn't understood.

Paul found himself in bed, fully dressed. There was a note from Robert on the bedside table.

'Dear Paul,

Were too much alike I'm afraid Paul. I've been lonely cors I have, don't think about it much now, well you cant brood all the time. I'd talk to yourself Paul if I were you, it helps you to keep going. With all that money you

could do what you like. Go on holiday, or hire a secretary, I suppose you have to find her something to do.
    Good luck Paul.
        All the best. Robert.'

# PART THREE

# PAUL AND MARY

# LIVING TOGETHER

Mary had lost her Post Office Book. She remembered standing
in a long queue to draw out a pound. The woman behind her
had a loud voice, deep like a man's, but with a posh accent.
The woman had sighed, and said, 'Oh, come on!' as if she
were the only person in the world. 'Come along, *do*! God,
what a time it takes, and all for one pound!' She was the only
woman in the world, and she wanted some stamps. 'If they
kept their machines filled up, there wouldn't be queues.' Mary
had told herself not to panic. She had as much right to be
attended to as the loud woman, who was now pushing at her
back. Mary had turned, near to tears, and asked the woman
not to push her. 'Well, don't take all day. There are others besides you.' She had then added, 'Me for one.'

They had laughed. The people who made up the four queues
had laughed, and Mary had taken her pound. It was not until
she had sat down in the park, and concentrated on the chry-
santhemums to stop herself crying, that she had discovered
the loss of the book.

At the Post Office, they did not remember her, since the man
who had served her was at lunch. 'There was a big lady pushing, and they laughed at me. I must have left it on the counter.
Don't you remember? I need it, you see, to live on.'

Nothing had been handed in, but they would be pleased to
take her name and address – well, just her name then – and
she could call again. People were usually honest with Post

Office property. No call for alarm; it happens all the time.

Every day for a week she spoke to the same man, and he never lost hope. But Mary did. She had weighed herself on a scale she found in Watford, which was broken, and weighed you for nothing. It told her that she weighed seven stone three. Mary had never known herself to be less than eight and a half stone. Her long walk to Fleetwood and back had slimmed her down. She did not mind missing meals. The food she had been able to afford (she could afford none now) no longer appealed to her. But she had noticed feeling faint, and had once had to sit down in Buxton High Street because she had come over giddy.

She had filled in a form to report her book missing, but the man had said that to issue a new one would take time, and would be all the slower because she did not have an address.

Mary walked slowly back to the address she did have, but could not give. At least that was something; she had arrived back in London to find the building workers still on strike. (In Manchester, she had read a newspaper which said 'BUILDERS REJECT OFFER. STRIKE IN TENTH WEEK'.) The planks were still loose. She had been able to take up residence in her luxury flat again.

She had walked a lot today, because every time she sat down, people – tourists mostly – would sit beside her, and she had felt forced to move on, self-conscious about her smell. It was not her imagination. Other things had been that, but not the smell. She had heard comments passed, seen people move away. She had gone to the Ladies, and scrubbed herself twice all over, bit by bit, first one part and then another, until she had cleansed her entire body, even the parts most vulnerable to smell, which annoyingly were the hardest parts to wash in a Public Convenience – but she had done it by taking the soap into one of the cubicles, and using the toilet as a hand-basin. Mary knew that what really made her smell were her clothes, because they had been slept in, sweated into, and sometimes stained.

She was going home earlier than usual, for it was not yet dark. Tiredness had brought on a careless feeling. She was too tired to think about the future or food. Soon she would have to give in. She would ask John, the vicar, for help. Since Albert no longer talked to her, there was no point in moving about. John had said he would help her. Perhaps she would do it to-morrow. If her book wasn't returned.

She was so tired. Mary thought that this must be the reason she was unable to move the plank. After trying again, she counted all the planks to the corner of the fence, just to be sure she was pressing the right one. At the corner, she saw the new sign, which said:

BEWARE!

GUARD DOGS ON PATROL

It was too late to walk to Willesden. Mary sat on the pavement where she was. If she were not careful, she would fall asleep. She could feel her eyes closing themselves. Her head slid to one side. She mustn't go to sleep. She must get up, and keep walking. Five minutes wouldn't hurt. They would give her time to think. She must plan ahead. If only she weren't so tired. Being hungry didn't matter; she was used to it; but you couldn't fight tiredness; it always won. Across the road was a policeman. Mary's eyes closed again. He had stopped, and was looking her way. She was sinking into the soft pavement; in a moment, she would be lying on her side. Traffic prevented the policeman from crossing the road. It was warm, and she could stretch out, and float, her feet tingling with relief. Traffic lights had halted the traffic, and the policeman started to cross. She could smell lilies. They were standing in a square black vase, carved out of marble. The smell was all around her. She could feel herself smiling. The smile seemed to bubble behind her face. It wanted to break into a laugh, but she wouldn't let it. It was her smile, and she wanted to make the most of it. A smile can last longer than a laugh, for a laugh tires you. Anyway, it's rude to laugh in a cemetery.

The policeman had crossed the road, and was standing near her. She had given in. There was no need to fight. She was going to sleep. He would tell her that she could; she had earned it. She had walked too far. He would lift her up (only seven stone three), and take her away, preferably in a van or car. He would tell the Alsatian to be quiet, and the Sergeant would have her put down. It was the best thing. She had earned it. They would find her Post Office Book, and bury her with Albert. There was room for her name on the vase. The lilies smelled strong. They must be an acquired smell, she thought.

'Don't stay there too long, will you, Mum?'

It was a hot evening in South Kensington. All the restaurants were extravagantly lighted, and people drifted up and down the pavements in the warm air. From the restaurants came smells of Italian, French, Chinese, Indian, Spanish and Greek food. From the five Steak Houses came smells of steak. Life was unfair. Mary had asked for very little. The gates into the garden of Onslow Square were kept locked.

'Frightened someone might steal the dog-shit!' She had become crude. She would become a crude old woman, who smelled. No, she would not become an old woman. She would not.

The benches in front of South Kensington Underground Station were full of tourists. If she could just find a seat next to one of them, then the tourist would soon move on. The pigeons were all asleep by now. They slept in the kitchens of Chinese restaurants, lovingly cared for by the cooks, or in some ventilation shaft, using the air of rich people. Mary sat on a low wall close to four Americans, and soon had their bench to herself. She would sit. If she lay on the bench she might be too conspicuous.

He did not recognize her. He had lain on top of her, poking his thing up her, and spilling his seed. He had called her names, and stopped Albert talking to her. He was sitting opposite on a bench, pretending to read a book, but looking from side to side, and he didn't recognize her. She must be sure, though. She had to be sure this time. In Manchester, he had turned out to be much too old, and in Hendon he had spoken with a foreign accent.

At eleven thirty, he closed his book, Coming Up For Air, and walked slowly the long way home. Mary followed him.

As he mounted the steps of Number a hundred and four, Onslow Square, Mary became sure.

'Don't you care what happens to your seed?'

Paul turned to see who was drunk. Mary was following him through the gate. 'I'm carrying your little one inside me, and you don't even say Hello.'

The line of people standing waiting for the last bus started to giggle.

'I'm sorry. I think you're mistaken.' He had not yet managed to find the key.

'I was lying on the grass, and you spilled yourself inside me.'

Four of the bus queue came to stand by Paul's gate.

'I don't understand you. I'm sorry.' He placed the key in the lock, and turned it.

Mary grabbed his arm. 'I can't look after it. I've lost my Savings Book.'

He could not escape her without pushing her, an old woman. More people had come to stand near the gate. The door was open now, but she was holding his arm, and seven people were watching.

'Why don't you come in where we can talk in private?' He felt he had scored a point, but it gave him little satisfaction.

He switched on the hall light, and they stared at each other.

Now she was no longer sure.

The face was like the one she remembered, but her memory of it was not as clear as it had been. Something about the eyes said that this was not the boy who had been so cocky.

If he could get away from her to a phone, he would ring for help. The police would know what to do.

'Are you sure you don't remember being naughty with me?'

He told her that he would not have forgotten if he had. She was not drunk. She had many smells, but alcohol was not one of them. 'Would you like me to telephone for someone to take you home?' She told him she was sorry. She had not eaten for days, and because of it, her eyes played tricks. It was possible she was mistaken.

'I could get you a taxi. I'll pay.' She was neither drunk nor mad. She was a tramp. But even tramps slept somewhere.

'The place I was sleeping in has been locked.'

He carried nothing but small change in his pocket when he went out at night. Robert had advised it. She would be offended by ten and a half pence.

'Can I offer you some supper?' She was leaning against the hall table, her eyes closed.

'That's very kind of you.'

Once upstairs, she might allow him to ring for help. 'I'm at the top, I'm afraid.'

'Oh, dear!'

'Here, let me help.'

'No. Don't.' She had grown to dislike being touched. 'I can manage, thank you.'

He tried to remember what there was to eat.

'Are there many more stairs?'

'No. We're home now.'

He was aware that he was speaking to her as if she were a

child. She was aware that she smelt, and that this was a house in which it would be noticeable.

Mary drank a glass of Macon, and picked at her Quiche Lorraine. Surely he was having her on, to say that he'd cooked it himself. And how rude he must consider her, not to be able to finish it. She would certainly do it justice in the morning, but at present she was finding it difficult to know where she was putting her fork, being so tired. Mary said she hoped he would not find her forward if she asked if she might sleep on his floor. The kitchen would do, since there was no carpet, but lino. She had no hope of finding anywhere else tonight. She assured him that it was simple tiredness, and begged him not to ring for an ambulance.

Paul showed Mary Richard's bedroom, and insisted that she use the bed. He explained where the bathroom was, and she promised she would make use of it.

When he woke her in the morning with tea, she was lying on the floor. The bed had been too soft. She had woken with a feeling of drowning. She hoped that he had not seen her clothes, which were drying in the bathroom. She had managed, she said, to rinse through one or two small pieces before she closed her eyes for good. It had been nice of him not to comment on the fact that she had a smell about her. She was hoping to get rid of it.

At breakfast, she insisted on finishing the bacon-and-egg pie she had left the night before. Paul made a mental note to stop calling it Quiche Lorraine. He ate a boiled egg slowly, and followed it with several slices of toast so that she would not see that he had finished, and stop eating.

Mary refused a sixth slice of toast. It was the largest meal she had eaten for ten months. She explained to him how the stomach shrinks without food, and he listened, wishing his would.

She didn't know his name, and she desired to use it.

'I'm sorry. I don't know your name.' Had he told her, and had she forgotten?

'Paul.'

She had decided to tell him about Albert. 'Mine's Watson, Mary Watson. I suppose I should have mentioned it last night.'

'My fault.'

They shook hands over the breakfast cups. It would have seemed odd, talking as she intended, to a stranger.

'I used to live in Willesden, Paul. In a flat.'

He was smiling at her, his eyes sad but interested. Now she had started, she would tell him everything. She had shouted at him in the street, in front of his neighbours; he had a right to know. Besides, it would help her sort things out, talking aloud to someone else. She might discover something she had missed, and he did seem interested.

'You see, Albert, who was my husband, died.'

The young man looked at her without blinking.

'He had a long and hard fight against his illness.'

His eyes seemed to see inside her head.

'An industrial accident, they called it.'

He was a handsome young man, old before his time.

'The doctor said he struggled hard to live.'

She would not get old. Not get crude.

Mary realized that the truth was sometimes difficult. It had not been an industrial accident, nor had Albert struggled to live. He had wanted to die, had given up the fight. But that was only half the truth. There had to be reasons, and Albert had never given them. In life or death.

Mary spoke of the cemetery. She spoke of her journey to Fleetwood. She spoke of being held down by three boys, while the fourth did things to her which had ended in his losing his iron control and spilling his seed inside her. It would have

180

been wrong to tell a stranger that she had fallen asleep on the grass verge, thinking of Albert, her body open for the boy to slide into.

He had listened without comment, his eyes never leaving hers. Now Mary was tired again. Talking out loud had not helped. On the contrary, she had lied, and lies confused her.

The young man sat there, waiting for more, but she had finished, ending with the Savings Book and the guard dogs. He had let his coffee get cold, hadn't touched it while she spoke.

She must make a move to stand, collect her washing from the bathroom, and walk to the Post Office. It would be open now. If the book had been found, she would take the Tube to Willesden.

'When's the baby due?'

Mary was so surprised by the question that she had to sit again to think.

'When did he plant his seed?'

For her life, she couldn't remember. 'It's difficult to work out. I wasn't counting the days.'

'I think you should stay here until you have to go into hospital.'


At three thirty, Harrod's delivered their firmest mattress, and took away the soft one. Mary was at the Post Office when they came, and so knew nothing about it.

The book had not been handed in. It had now been missing a fortnight, but the man to whom Mary spoke said, 'Never say die.' Paul had given her a key, and she moved it around in her pocket. She had spent the morning washing every item in her bundle twice, including her wedding dress. A shirt and a pair of Richard's trousers had been found for her, so that she could wash what she had been wearing.

She had agreed, after much argument, to stay for a day or

two in order to do her laundry. She had no intention of staying longer, and imposing herself. She had lied about Albert,
lied because she had expected to walk out of the flat after
breakfast, and never see the kind young man again. Now, as
she entered a shop with five pounds and the list he had given
her, she wished she had told the truth.

Paul had given her a short shopping-list, and suggested that
they have dinner early, and then watch a little television. Although they had worked out that she could not be more
than three months pregnant, the sooner she started going to
bed early, the better. *

# A DAY AT A TIME

At the end of four days, Mary had cleaned the flat completely twice. Her clothes and bundle had been ironed and aired, and in some cases repairs had been made and buttons replaced.

There was now no reason for her to stay.

Albert had not been in touch. Twice she had felt that he was about to say something, but he had not.

Paul had bought two new cookery books, and experimented on her with all kinds of new tastes, and Mary, who had a lot of weight to make up, and was feeding two, had, as she put it, eaten like a horse without a nose-bag.

She had continued to sleep on the floor. Now that the bed was firm, she dreamed of falling off its edge, and so she had returned to the comfortably thick carpet. At night she left the curtains open, so that she woke early, and was able to get back into bed before Paul knocked at the door with tea.

The four days had passed quickly. They had both worked hard during the day, and in the evening they had sat sipping sherry and watching the television. Mary had not asked about Paul's background. It didn't seem the thing to do. And Paul did not intend to repeat the mistake he had made with Robert. They had talked about the flat, and Mary cleaning it, about Paul's cooking, and about what they saw on television. Mary was fascinated by the colour, so they watched that, regardless of the programme. And on each of those nights, Mary had gone to bed (or to floor) at nine thirty.

On the fifth day, there was nothing for Mary to do. Paul

had spent most of the night trying to think of a new project, but when he took Mary her tea in the morning she was already dressed, and looking for string to tie her bundle. Paul explained that he always forgot to save string, but that if she would help him do the shopping they could get some then. Mary produced four bits she had found, but none of them was long enough or strong enough. String was very important, she said; she liked it to be perfect. She had thrown away the string she arrived with, because it smelled.

The morning was spent in Paul's pottering around the kitchen, making the longest shopping-list he could think of, and Mary's cleaning all the shoes she could find, including Richard's.

After lunch, they armed themselves with large shopping bags, and headed towards Sainsbury's in the King's Road. As they walked along a row of tiny terraced houses, each one painted a different colour, Paul suddenly looked up at the blue sky, and the words 'National Trust' came into his mind.

While they unpacked the shopping, which was mostly tinned baby-foods and the two balls of strong but soft white string, Paul told Mary what they were to do next day. Neither made any mention of the baby-foods.

Inspecting the house took them no more than an hour, but it had served its purpose. Mary had stayed another day. As they were leaving, Mary asked Paul if he'd noticed how yellow some of the paintwork had been allowed to get. Paul said he had, and Mary went on to say that it had made her think that his living-room could do with a new coat of paint or paper. Mary said that the only reason she had mentioned it was that she enjoyed decorating, and had always been the one to do it in the past. Paul told her that it was out of the question to stand on ladders in her condition, and the room was much bigger than she thought. Mary said that she would take it easy, working an hour, then resting an hour.

The ceiling was not a high one, and she could almost reach it by standing on tip-toe. Paul agreed that the ceiling was not high, but said that he would only consider Mary's suggestion if she allowed him to pay her in money with which to buy baby clothes. He remembered that he had begun by decorating the flat, and ended in staying ten years. Mary wished him to realize that it would take at least a week.

On the way home, they bought some chocolate cake for tea, and Paul said that he would not eat bread from now on.

As they ate the cake, they looked at the walls. Paul had painted them two months before Richard's death, choosing a pale yellow to match the curtains. They talked of what to do. Mary asked Paul what he would like done, and Paul said he had no idea, and would rely on her judgement; decorating was only fun if one had picked the materials oneself. Mary said that their tastes might be different, and Paul laughed, and said he had none. Mary thought a nice wallpaper might make a change. Paul agreed.

Next day, Paul looked at the thin cheap wallpaper, on which large violet harebells were surrounded by wreaths of ivy, and said how much he liked it. It would give the room that homely touch it needed. Mary added that it would make a nice background for all those big paintings, and returned most of the thirty pounds he had given her, saying that she would ask for some of it back when she started on the bathroom.

When she had finished the living-room, Paul took Mary to look round Osterley Park. At a certain stage of their inspection of the house, he pointed to the ceiling and said 'That's Adam.' Mary could see nobody at all on the ceiling, but thought it only polite to reply 'Goodness!' For the rest of the time, they discussed the possibilities of their own bathroom. Paul said that he would like it to be plain and simple, and Mary said that she had always fancied Duck-Egg Blue.

After a visit to Ham House (which Mary found very dark), the kitchen received a washable paper, with hanging pheasants and copper saucepans painted on it, and when she returned from Syon House, she began to cover Richard's bedroom with pink roses. On the day that the last rose blotted out the final square inch of Richard's hand-printed William Morris wallpaper, they had been living together four weeks, and calculated that Mary must be approximately four months pregnant.

Two days later, Mary fell off a chair, while trying to push bundles of old magazines into the attic. Paul helped her from the floor. Nothing was broken, and she was quite able to walk, but Paul mumbled something about miscarriage, and confined her to bed.

After washing the dust of the attic from her hands and face, Mary sat up in bed, wearing the night-dress and bedjacket Paul had bought, while the television set was removed from the living-room, and placed before her bed.

Now, at nine every morning, fruit juice was brought instead of tea, since tea now made her feel sick. Mary, who had spent the night on the floor, would be sitting up in bed. While sipping the juice slowly, she would read the *Daily Mirror*, which Paul had ordered specially. Paul meanwhile would prepare for Mary egg and bacon, with tomatoes or mushrooms, four slices of toast, and two cups of weak coffee, since strong coffee was assumed to be bad for the baby's heart. Paul himself would eat Ryvita with a lightly boiled egg, and then have a quick bath.

After the bath, breakfast would be cleared away, while Mary listened to Jimmy Young, or read one of the many magazines. The day after the accident, Paul had gone to the bookstall at South Kensington Station, and bought *Woman*, *Woman's Own*, *Woman's Realm*, *Woman's Weekly*, *The*

*Lady, Home and Garden, House and Garden, Country Life, Queen, Vogue* and *Elle* (for its pictures).

The washing-up done, Mary would be led around the flat on Paul's arm, in and out of every bedroom twice. She would then be taken to the bathroom, where she would be asked by Paul if she had all she needed. Paul would stand outside the door in case of emergency, and busy himself with something useful, such as shelling peas, stringing beans, or making out the day's shopping-list.

Once she was safely out of the bath and drying herself, Paul would rush into the bedroom and remake Richard's bed. The sheets were changed every other day, to avoid a build-up of biscuit crumbs. When she was respectable, Mary would knock on the inside of the bathroom door, and Paul would lead her back to bed, where she would read until Paul had done the shopping, and was home again to give her lunch.

Lunch was usually uncooked, or something which had been precooked the night before while Mary was watching television. Eating it together on the side of Richard's bed, they would plan Mary's afternoon. Paul would scan the *Radio Times* and *T.V. Times* to help her decide between *Watch With Mother* or *Racing From Sandown Park*. Racing was more fun, since she and Paul would pick four horses each, and he would run off after lunch to put fifty pence each way on them.

When the horses Mary had chosen won – which was not often, since she chose them simply for their names – the money was put into the hand of a black man. The man was then wound up until he ate the coins with a loud clanging noise. This always made them laugh. The money was to be left inside the smiling black man's tummy until Mary's baby was old enough to get it out.

Sometimes there would be no racing, and Paul would come back after washing up the lunch things, to sit with her, and play games. He had bought a large variety of these, and they had a try at most of them except dominoes. Paul thought dominoes to be quite a good game for two people, but Mary never wanted to play it. He taught her, as Richard had taught him, to play Bezique. They played for two pence a point, and Mary nearly always won, but since they kept a running score, money never changed hands.

The days passed slowly for Mary. She submitted to the routine because it seemed to give Paul so much pleasure, but she grew to dislike it more and more. She could perfectly well get up and walk about, and did so when Paul was asleep. Walking or working stopped her from thinking too much. If she thought, it was usually of the baby or Albert. The first thought frightened her; the second worried and depressed her. If she was busy, she could go for hours with nothing in her head.

She had never been one for magazines, except for the page where women who needed advice or help sent in their letters to be read out. One day, while Paul was washing up, Mary got so bored that she wrote to Evelyn Home, telling her about Albert. She did not mention the episode of the boy by the road-side, or the fact that she was now pregnant. She simply explained that Albert had stopped talking to her, and asked what she should do. Miss Home had said, in answer to one of her correspondents, that there was nothing so painful it couldn't be shared, and that there was always someone else in the same boat, so Mary signed the letter 'Shipmate', and asked Paul to post it when he went shopping. She did not think it proper to give an address. There was no reply.

Paul armed himself with books on pre-natal care, including one called *Natural Birth by Sister Pratt*, and Mary was given exercises in addition to her walks round the flat. Certain muscles were going to be called upon to do a lot of work, so they must not be allowed to get slack.

Exercise, and rest. Rest, then exercise. Lying on her back,

and bringing her knees up over her head as far as possible, then rolling from side to side, Mary was able to cast from her mind all depressing thoughts, and concentrate on staying on the bed. For this exercise, she was allowed to wear a pair of Richard's pyjamas.

For relaxation (an exercise she thought unnecessary, since she was lying in bed already), Paul asked Mary to lie on her stomach, one arm above her head, the opposite knee bent. After half an hour, she might change sides and limbs. Mary hated this exercise, since the whole point of it was to relax, and she found it gave her cramp. Remembering never to bend, but always to squat with knees pointed outwards, was another thing she found difficult.

She continued to put on weight, as the book said she should. Also she developed desires for odd mixtures of food, as the book said she might. Mary's desires were for pickles dipped in jam, and oatmeal biscuits spread with Marmite.

Paul began to wonder at what stage the baby would begin to kick, and be felt by Mary. When he asked her if she had felt the baby kick, she looked so frightened that he decided not to refer to it again. He had developed a longing to feel the baby's movement himself. The urge to reach out and place his hand on Mary's stomach was so strong that he found it hard to take his eyes from where he assumed the baby to be. Finally he told Mary that he was supposed to keep a check on her size, and, with the help of a tape measure, he was able to press his fingers against various parts of her stomach, hoping that the baby would respond to pressure.

After a while, Mary found that she was unable to sleep at night. She told Paul that this was because she spent all day in bed. Paul answered by saying that she and Baby needed all the rest they could get, and that if she were to get up now it would undo all the good which had been done by her convalescence of the last six weeks, and she and Baby might find it difficult to get through a safe delivery. He explained that 'delivery' meant the moment when Baby arrived. Then he relented and said that he had not meant to say 'safe' but 'comfortable'. Mary, who had learned in hospital that 'discomfort' was the doctors' word for 'pain' promised that she would try to empty her mind, and concentrate on sleep.

Another week passed, and Mary continued not to sleep. Paul had given her more exercises, and allowed her to spend five minutes walking round the flat twice a day, once in the morning before her bath, and once last thing at night.

Mary started to take longer in the bathroom. She would lie in the sunken bath, moving her arms and legs as though swimming backwards, and thinking about Albert. She wondered if he could see her in these new surroundings, and what, if he were to make a comment, it would be. The first time she had come into this room, she had been unable to find the bath, thinking this large square in the floor to be something to do with a shower. Now she moved around in it, as if it were her own. Now she smelled like a chemist's shop, and washed her hair twice a week with shampoo. It deserved some kind of comment, but Albert made none.

When she had been in the bath for half an hour, Paul would shout to ask if she was all right, even though he could hear her splashing the water about. Mary would think of him, sitting on a stool outside the door, having finished shelling the peas, but unable to move in case she fell or fainted. She would shout that she was sorry; she had been dreaming. And Paul would shout again to tell her not to hurry, because he had not yet finished his work. Mary would smile to imagine sacks of unshelled peas stacked against the bathroom door, and Paul buried in a mound of shells, and she would step like Cleopatra from her sunken bath, thoroughly soaked.

Drying herself also took longer now. It was not simply that there was more of her to dry. A couple of inches here and there could not account for ten minutes spent in front of the full-length mirror. Where once Richard had watched himself expand, Mary stood sideways, and pushed her stomach out, and tried to visualize what was inside it. Somewhere in there was a tiny (she hoped tiny) baby, a human being which was half Mary and half someone Mary didn't know, and had only seen the back of, running away. He had looked like Paul, though. She was sure of it.

Every day it was getting bigger. Every day she drank a pint of milk to strengthen its bones and teeth. Every day she was eating crusts to make its hair curl. Every day she drank fruit juice to protect it from colds, and swallowed vitamin pills, which gave her constipation, and forced her to take laxatives of a gentle sort, which would not scour it. It would arrive with nails on both fingers and toes because she had chewed apples and kept off the gin, which she didn't like anyway. (Paul had given up alcohol too.) The exercises she did twice a day would enable it to crawl, and later, walk. After its 'delivery', it would be fed on what Prince Charles and Princess Anne had been fed on, but for now it was to nourish itself on her, and the pickles and jam, Paul said, would give it strength of character.

Mary left the bathroom on Paul's arm, wondering what it felt like to be kicked, and if, when the baby kicked, it was trying to say something.

It started with a heartbeat. Then the heartbeat was a slight kick, and the kick was lower down. In his stomach. His stomach was swelling because of the kick. Expanding. Being pushed out by a tapping that was growing, the kicking of a foot no bigger than a toenail. As big as a toenail, but with toenails. They were the size of tomato pips. They were growing. Everything was growing. The foot, its toenails, the strength of the kick, his stomach, and the hollow inside it.

Measuring himself was impossible. Thirty-six inches became thirty-eight inches, then forty-one. From nowhere, a longer tape measure was handed to him.

The kicking began to echo, the next blow arriving before the first had died.

Paul lifted his knees above his head, and rolled first to the left side, then the right. By rolling, he reached the end of the bed. The bed was not growing. Trying to lie on his stomach, with alternate arm and leg bent, he found that, because of the size of his stomach, his head and legs were suspended in mid-air, with nothing to rest against.

The tape said he measured a hundred and forty-four inches.

Suddenly the kicking stopped. Silence. Paul waited.

Nothing. Silence. No heartbeat. No kick. No pulse. Silence.

Paul moved from his side to his back. The bed groaned. Again silence. The sheets were cold with sweat.

A sharp spear of pain shot up his back passage, and buried itself in his back.

Silence. Paul's legs parted themselves. Silence.

Paul's back, buttocks and thighs reared and lifted off the mattress. The spear was being dragged out slowly, a millimetre at a time. As it came, it was cutting, tearing his insides. Kidneys. Intestines. Bowels. Cavities for waste food. Shelves of membrane, which normally expand and contract, kept themselves tense as the spear bit through.

Then the water broke.

Everything was going. Flooding away. The purge had begun. Nothing could be left inside after such force. Paul saw gallons of acid water gushing from him onto the floor, soaking through the mattress and blankets, lapping under and around the bed.

Finally, with the last and largest gush, the baby shot out like a harpoon fired from a cannon, with the umbilical cord flying through the air behind it. The cord seemed to reel out endlessly, as the baby bobbed up and down in a sea of afterbirth.

Paul bit through the cord, and woke up.

She was unable to keep still. She would find a comfortable position, then suddenly she would start to itch, or a pain would develop like the cramp she sometimes got from crossing her legs for too long.

Usually she slept on her side. One side or the other; it made no difference. Before, it had depended on whether she was lying on a slope, or which way the wind was blowing, but on either side, she usually got to sleep. Until now.

Mary stood up, and moved to the stretch of carpet at the other side of Richard's bed.

After a while she itched again. This time it was something crawling up the inside of her leg.

She switched on the light, and saw nothing. A moth moved from the lamp-shade to the wardrobe, and she felt obliged to kill it before trying to sleep again.

Half an hour later, she sat on the edge of the bed, having given up all hopes of sleep. It was three o'clock. She would read until morning.

At four thirty, she needed to use the bathroom. On her way back, she passed Paul's bedroom door. There was no sound. Even pulling the chain (which was not a chain, but a lever) had not wakened him.

Mary took one pound and thirty-two pence from the stomach of the black man who ate money.

At any moment he could wake, and stop her.

The soft but strong white string was kept in a cupboard by the kitchen sink. She found it, and measured three yards, stretching it out at arm's length from her nose.

At any moment he could wake, and stop her.

Sprinkling talcum powder inside her shoes, and tying her hair back with a ribbon, she tried to decide what to wear. The morning would be cold, but then it might get warm later, and that would mean re-packing the bundle.

Mary listened again at Paul's door. At any moment he could wake, and stop her.

Back in her room, she began to tidy it, putting the blankets on the bed. There was no need to arrange it as if it had been slept in. Today was a day for changing the sheets. She felt sure that she heard him getting out of bed while she was putting things in drawers and closing cupboards.

Almost an hour passed from the moment that she made the decision to the moment when she opened the door of the flat, and walked downstairs. On the steps outside the house, she stood for a moment to take in the cold. She had not made a good choice in clothes, and he had not stopped her.

A dead pigeon lay in the road.

Mary walked to the triangle in front of South Kensington Station, and sat for a few minutes. She was tired. She must remember her condition. It had rained during the night; the seat was damp. She moved on when the cold began to strike. Suddenly she was hungry. At seven thirty, the South Kensington Restaurant (or Cafeteria) would open. But now it was not yet six.

The morning was cold. It seemed to get colder. Placing her bundle on the doorstep (why did it seem heavier now?) she untied the carefully knotted string. A police car slowed down as it passed. The two cardigans were at the bottom of the bundle. Silly to have put them there. She wore the green one over the red, because the red had more buttons. The bundle had to be tied again, but her fingers were too cold to work. Mary breathed on them, and made a bow.

The bundle was lighter, and she would be warmer. The

police car came back, and the policeman waved. Mary turned the corner, and met Paul.

'I thought I'd go for a walk.'

'I thought I would.'

They walked together, Mary setting the pace, and Paul fitting his stride to match hers. Their footsteps echoed in the empty street. Although they were walking without destination, doing it for the exercise, physical and mental, they moved with an urgency.

It was a grey morning. Almost everything was grey. Banks of heavy cloud hid the sky, leaving no blue in which to dress a sailor.

Paul concentrated on the sounds their steps made. His made two sounds, *click* then *tap*, *click* then *tap*, heel then toe, while Mary made a single sound, *flap*, putting her full weight behind each stride, *flap* stride *flap*.

He was not cold, except for his face. He wore an overcoat, and buried his hands in his pockets.

'Can I carry that?'

'It's not heavy.'

*Flap, click, tap.*

There was no use in offering his coat; she would not accept it. His face tingled, bitten by the cold, a pleasant feeling. It would do him good. His nose began to run. He imagined that she must be used to the cold, hardened to it, for she simply wore a cotton dress and two cardigans.

'Are you warm enough?'

'I will be soon.'

*Flap, click, tap.*

Stacked on top of one another in some of the doorways were cardboard boxes and dustbins full of waste paper and last night's Plat du Jour.

A sleek young cat walked beside them both for a while,

stopping here and there to examine the refuse, then leaping and running to catch up.

*Flap, click, tap.*

An electric milk-cart waited patiently for the lights to change, although there was no other traffic in sight. As red changed to amber, it droned gracefully round the corner, its bottles rattling quietly against the plastic crates.

*Flap, click, tap.*

They turned left with the milk-cart, and were heading home. Both of them sensed it.

'Let me take it for a while.' He took the bundle from her back, allowing her to slip fingers red with cold into the pockets of the green cardigan.

*Flap, click, tap.*

'So this is what it's like?'

She was not sure what he meant.

'To carry your home on your back.'

They had arrived at Onslow Square. The dead pigeon still lay on its side in the road, its legs sticking stiffly out in front of it. A trickle of dark red blood rolled like toffee down its chest. Its eyes were screwed up tight.

On the roof of the building opposite, they saw another pigeon, hopping backwards and forwards on the same four feet of ledge. The bird made a long drawn-out cooing noise, and seemed to be throwing its voice down into the road, so that it was as if the sound came from the dead pigeon's slightly open beak. It was not the gurgling sound of a pigeon searching for food, but a low painful moan, which at that time of the morning and in an empty street, was sinister and disturbing.

When Mary lifted the dead bird by its stiff legs, and placed it through the railings into the bushes of Onslow Square, the pigeon on the roof flew away.

'I wasn't running away, Paul. I'm sure I would have come back.'

'I dreamt I was having your baby. Then I went for a walk. I wasn't following you.' He lowered her bundle onto the doorstep. 'You're not a prisoner, Mary. If you feel like one, I think you'd be right to leave.'

'I don't want to leave just yet, if it's all right for me to stay.'

'Shall we have breakfast?'

'Yes.'

'Have you ever been to Crystal Palace?'

'No.'

'I thought we'd take a bus this afternoon.'

'That would be nice.'

The following morning, Mary rose first, and took Paul tea in bed. He was up before she could prepare breakfast, but allowed her to lay the table, showing her where things were kept. He told her that if she really wished it, they could take it in turns to make his tea, prepare her fruit juice, and cook them both breakfast.

That evening, the television was moved back into the living-room, and by the end of the first week Mary was cooking at least half their meals.

In the second week, she suggested that they could save in laundry bills by investing in a washing machine with a spin-drier. Mary had always longed for one of those machines which arrive with a packet of washing powder inside it, recommended by the makers. When Paul asked where the clothes would hang to finish drying, Mary replied that the kitchen was an ideal place to have a clothes line, as the heat from the oven was then used twice.

Paul invested in a Hoover Keymatic, identical to the one his mother had bought. Removing a beautiful cluster of onions he had bought at the door from a Breton, he tied off one end of a piece of rope, and led the other end across the small kitchen just above their heads to the shelves of Spanish stoneware. He soon found that working in the kitchen while the machine was switching itself on and off after every one of its many activities was impossible. He would try to find out from Mary when she intended using it, and make that his time to do the shopping – slowly. Or he would lie, soaking himself in the bath, which was at the other end of the flat, waiting for the final automatic switch to tell him that he could start to dry himself.

The machine was used to wash something every other day, if only handkerchiefs, and while the machine washed and whirled, Mary polished all the furniture with a polish that smelled of roses. Every day she hoovered and dusted, and once a week she cleaned the windows and the oven.

Most of the curtains had been sent away to be cleaned, since they were too long to dry in the kitchen, but the living-room curtains had been washed in the machine, and dyed violet to match the harebells which now brightened the living-room.

Meanwhile both Paul and Mary continued their exercises, Paul doing his to strengthen his stomach muscles. The exercises were performed twice a day, immediately after breakfast and last thing at night. Mary had less than twelve weeks to go. She no longer continued to put on weight, but Paul said that this was as it should be.

In the centre of the living-room was a space just large enough for two bodies to lie down flat, and roll from side to side. They both did exactly the same exercises. Doing them together, they were able to become slightly competitive, and this made for a greater effort. Since the exercises recommended by Sister Pratt made Paul's stomach muscles ache, he assumed that they must be doing him good.

When Mary had less than nine weeks to go, Paul thought

it was time to start Sister Pratt's Distracting Exercises. The Sister's idea was that by concentrating hard on something else while the baby is being born, the mother can remain unaware of the tremendous pain she is suffering. The Sister suggested watching a good T.V. play or a variety show during the early stages of labour, reading poetry or prose (but not aloud), and counting in threes – three, six, nine, twelve, fifteen, eighteen, and so on – which is harder than it seems when the patient gets to around three hundred and thirty-three. Presumably, if the delivery proved to be a long one, an all-time record could be set up for the first mother to reach four million.

Tapping out a rhythm on her thighs, and watching her fingers carefully, Mary silently mouthed the words of 'Please Release Me, Let Me Go, For I Don't Love You Any More.' Paul, who was by now able to read her lips, stopped her at the end of the first verse, and asked her to choose another song, so as not to tempt providence. It was important, he said, to practise a new song with a different rhythm every day. Mary began again with 'Anyone Who Had a Heart Could Look at Me, and Know that I Love You.' Since these were the only words of the song that she could remember, she repeated them thirty-seven times until Paul told her that she had been tapping for three minutes, and could stop. On alternate days, she practised with alternate hands, so that, on whichever side she found herself in labour, she could tap away the pain with ease.

With only eight weeks to go, Mary returned from shopping carrying a large roll of floral material. She explained to Paul that she had found it reduced to nineteen pence a yard, and had thought at once what pretty cushion covers it would make for the living-room. The floral cotton clashed violently with the harebells on the wallpaper, but Paul agreed that, at nineteen pence a yard, Mary would have been silly to pass it by.

When Mary gave him the change from the shopping, he

asked her how she had paid for the ten yards of material. She said that she had remembered her Post Office Book while out shopping, and had gone to see the man who never lost hope. The old book had not been handed in, but the form she had filled out to report its loss had been through all the right channels, and a new book issued.

'Been waiting here for some time, this had. Course if you'd left an address or phone, you'd have had it a lot sooner. Only takes a day or two usually. But with yours, there were complications.'

'I'm sorry.'

'Sign here. Done it? Right. Yes, well they questioned the signature on your last withdrawal form. This looks all right though. Expect you were in a rush or something.'

After discussing her financial affairs with Paul, Mary returned to the man who never lost hope, and told him she wished to close her account, and invest in a Building Society with interest at eight per cent. Paul had also told Mary that even at the two and a half per cent which the Post Office had given her she could have afforded to spend another ten shillings a week. Mary insisted that if that was the case, she could now afford to pay him one pound fifty a week for her keep, and reluctantly he agreed.

The next day, Paul took Mary to his bank, and introduced her to the manager as his aunt. Mary left the bank, a small but valued investor.

# A CERTAIN STYLE

Seven weeks more. They had consulted a calendar, and tried to work out the exact day, but since Mary could not remember whether the spilling of seed had happened on a Thursday, Friday or Saturday, it was a little difficult. However, she did remember that it had been a Sunday when she arrived in Fleetwood, so it had to be one of those days.

Paul managed, after much difficulty, to obtain a one-inch Ordnance Survey map of Fleetwood and the surrounding district. He asked Mary the name of the village near which the spilling had happened, but she could remember only that the village contained a small Co-Op, and Co-Ops unfortunately were not marked on the map. The road by which she had sat waiting for the ambulance had been called either Lilac or Rhododendron Road. Paul thought 'Rhododendron Road' sounded unlikely. They could find Lilac Lane and Lilac Walk, but no Lilac Road, and Mary remembered that, on the sign across from where she sat, the word 'ROAD' had been carefully blocked out with chalk, and a rude word substituted. Paul became even more sure that the name of the road must have been 'Lilac'. In front of most of the rude words he knew, 'Lilac' and 'Rhododendron' were both unlikely, but 'Lilac' less so.

Using the side of Paul's ruler that had eighths marked on it, they measured south from Fleetwood, and narrowed the possible villages down to three. Then they did sums, allowing for the time it must have taken her to get through Blackpool, and for the delay caused by the business of the trapped man.

Another consideration was that, after the spilling of seed, Mary moved much more slowly, necessarily so, with her stomach pushed forward, and trying not to fall.

Having done their sums, they came to the conclusion that Mary must have arrived in Fleetwood three days after the seed had been spilt. Therefore the baby had been conceived on a Thursday. Mary said that Thursday's child was full of woe, but Paul replied that he had been taught that Thursday's child had far to go, and anyway the rhyme applied to the day the child was born, not the day it was conceived.

They had discovered the right day, but as they had calculated Paul had become less and less confident that Mary's memory could be relied upon. They had the right day, but it might be in the wrong week.

Meanwhile something else also troubled him. While they were shopping one day, Mary had asked Paul to wait outside while she went into a chemist's shop. When she came out, carrying a small brown-paper parcel, he asked her what she had bought. She told him that it was 'women's things', and that she had got out of the habit of buying proper ones because of the expense. And on the day after, she excused herself from exercises, saying that it was her 'bad day'.

Paul knew, or thought he knew, that the sign of a woman's being pregnant was that her periods stopped. Yet Mary was having periods, even though she was pregnant. Could she be mistaken about the pregnancy? Beginning slowly and tactfully, Paul asked Mary at what point she had known she was pregnant, and if she had felt the baby move yet. (He remembered to avoid using the word 'kick'.) He also asked her whether anything other than the tea he had brought her in bed had made her feel sick.

Mary replied that she had known shortly after the spilling had happened. She was sure that the boy had lost his iron control, because he had remained inside her until she had removed his thing, which was sticky. She did indeed feel something inside her tummy. If she lay very still, it would bump. Then of course the baby talked to her.

This was a reference to the fact that Mary had taken to farting frequently. It had first happened as she and Paul sat together on Richard's bed, eating their dinner. She had tried to control the fart, and release it without noise, but it had made a noise anyway. A loud noise. For a while they had not been able to look at each other, and Paul had coughed, and dragged his plate across the tray in order to try to re-create the loud noise. But they both knew what had really happened. After the silence, Mary had said 'Excuse me. I think Baby's trying to tell me not to eat too fast.' Then they had both giggled, and Paul had said that he had been trying to tell her that for days, and that clearly it needed Baby to complain before action was taken. Ever since then, Mary had farted freely, and they had laughed, and said 'Sorry, Baby.'

Clearly Mary was very sure that she was expecting a baby, and she should know. Nevertheless, there were the periods. Paul decided to consult Sister Pratt's book again. He flicked over his favourite passages. 'You have three holes at the base of your body. The opening nearest the backbone leads to the bowels, the one at the front leads to the bladder, while the middle one leads to the vaginal canal, which in turn leads to the womb. Try not to get these openings confused.' Nothing about periods. He looked up 'periods' in the index. 'Placenta' ... 'Pre-Natal Care' ... 'Pubic Hair' ... No, nothing. Paul knew that Mary could not be pregnant, and continue to have periods, yet she was pregnant, and she was having them. The page slipped under his fingers, and he found himself looking at the index entries for the letter 'B'. Out of the page there came a single word. He was staring at it. The word was 'Bleeding' and after it were the words, 'danger of'.

He would have to consult a doctor; there was no help for

it. Clearly he should have done so before. Why hadn't he? Sister Pratt had assumed that all her mothers were in touch with a doctor, midwife or the Ante-Natal Clinic; she had constantly referred to one or the other. Paul had not read out any of these references to Mary. After all, Ante-Natal Clinics were optional. Not all women used them, and with the help of Sister Pratt he and Mary had formed their own. Mary had told him of her experiences with doctors. They had not been happy. She had mentioned more than once the time she had been asked to count backwards and name the Prime Minister.

He had followed Sister Pratt's book closely, and they had done everything together without upsetting Mary. Now they would have to bring in outsiders to disrupt their life together. The book had said that it was a criminal offence not to inform the authorities when a woman started in labour. Could it also be an offence not to let them know of a pregnancy? If Mary had not accosted him that night, she might have had her baby in a hedge somewhere. Doubtless it would have died – perhaps been born dead – and she would have buried it in a field, or someone's back garden under a gooseberry bush.

He sat in a chair in the waiting-room of the doctor's surgery near Kensington Church Street, trying to rehearse over and over in his head his excuses for not having sent Mary to an Ante-Natal Clinic. Always he would get to the word 'because', and then stop. 'I didn't make Mary go to an Ante-Natal Clinic, because ...' The doctor's Surgery and residence were in an old house on three floors. The waiting-room, which was on the ground floor, was filled with very beautiful but very old furniture. Six armchairs surrounded a square of Persian carpet which was so old that if one looked carefully at the threadbare patches, one could read the newspapers underneath. 'I didn't suggest that Mary should go to an Ante-Natal Clinic because ...'

All the chairs made a noise. The man who sat in an elegant stick-back made it click every time he turned a page of his old but perfectly preserved *Tatler*. Paul's chair was covered in cracked leather, and it sighed heavily as he stood to reach for a copy of *Hare and Hound*.

'Mary *didn't know about Ante-Natal Clinics, and I didn't tell her because* ...' '*I didn't come to see you before about this matter, because* ...' Having seen his last patient out by the front door, Dr MacDonald poked his head into the waiting-room, and announced to Paul that he was next. This was the doctor Paul had called at the time of Richard's heart attack. In all the years before and months since Richard's death, Paul had never needed to consult him.

'It's Paul, isn't it?'

'That's right.'

'Not been here before, have you?'

'No.'

'Too healthy by half. How am I supposed to make ends meet if you're never ill? Might try a bit harder, you know. Develop some nice psychological complaint. Then we can just sit down and talk about it. After that, I'll pass you on to a friend of mine for an even bigger fee, and he'll send me a bottle of some very dry sherry. No? Pity! There's no *style* left in doctoring any more.' He pulled the word 'style' out of his chatter, so that it clicked off his tongue like a cro-quet ball being chopped over its opponent and through the final hoop.

By now they had climbed the stairs, and reached the sur-gery. It seemed to Paul that 'style' was all about him. 'Sit down, Paul. We must make your first visit a comfortable one. Now, what's the problem?' The walls were covered with red velvet, and in the corner stood a screen inlaid with mother-of-pearl. 'I *didn't send Mary to an Ante-Natal Clinic because* ...' 'What can I do for you?' A skeleton clock, which looked like Coventry Cathedral under a glass dome, ticked reverently. '*The reason I didn't make Mary go to an Ante-Natal Clinic was because ...*'

'Well, it's rather difficult to explain.'

'Try. I doubt if you could surprise me, you know.'

'You see, I met this woman ...'

The doctor's expression became watchful, but sympathetic. 'Go on.'

'She'd nowhere to stay. I've been looking after her. She'd had a bad experience with some boys on the roadside.'

'This woman is actually living with you?'

'She'd been ... well "walking about", I think you'd call it. I didn't send her to a Clinic because ...' Paul found some words to follow the 'because'. 'I hadn't the heart to.'

'This problem you're trying to tell me about, Paul. Is it a consequence of having had sex?'

'Yes.'

'A lot of nonsense is talked about this sort of thing. Folk-lore and such. You mustn't be frightened of it. It's all in the day's work to me. First, is there a discharge?'

'Yes, I think there is.'

'We'd better be sure, hadn't we?'

'Yes.'

'Drop your trousers, then, will you?' The doctor moved away swiftly, and began to wash his hands. Style was style, but time was money.

'I'm sorry. I'm afraid I'm not very good at explaining myself.'

'No matter, Paul. You're not the only one. I blame the parents, you know. There's so much misinformation about.'

'But –'

'If they didn't scare their kids, telling them how awful and terrible sex is, then some of them might come and consult an expert. Like me.'

'That's why I came. For advice.'

'And I'm glad you did. You seem to be having trouble with those trousers. Is it painful to pee? You know – sharp, like passing broken glass.'

'No.'

'Let me have a look.' The doctor dried his hands on a red towel. 'Does either of your balls ache? Or both?'

Paul suddenly remembered that his balls did ache. At least, the left one did. Sometimes in the cinema, or sitting on a bus, he would want to get up and walk about, or better still, rearrange all his private parts so that they were dressed on the other side. Anyway, the simplest thing now was to answer the question.

'Well, yes, they do sometimes.'

'Ah! Right! Get those down.'

Paul lowered his trousers.

'Feet slightly apart. There! Does it hurt now?' The doctor was gently bouncing Paul's left ball in the palm of his hand.

'No. Not now.'

'Let's have a go at this chap.' The doctor squeezed the end of Paul's penis, causing great pain. Paul flexed all his leg muscles, especially those behind his knees, and bit his tongue. Now the doctor looked through a magnifying glass at the hole in Paul's penis, as he squeezed harder, and twisted it round.

'Not a drop. Not a trickle. Not even a pinch. And you say it doesn't hurt to pee?' The doctor dropped Paul's penis, and, as it hit his balls, he thought he felt the beginnings of a slight ache.

'No.'

'We'll give you a jab, just to be on the safe side.'

The doctor took from a drawer a cellophane packet, opened it, and removed from it a disposable syringe.

'Turn round, Paul, and lean over the bed. No, on second

thoughts, lie on the bed, and face the wall.' Paul did so. 'That's right. Bend your knees a bit more.'

Paul heard the doctor put down the syringe, and unwrap a packet of disposable rubber gloves. A moment later, cream was applied to Paul's anus, and a finger pushed up. When the finger reached as far as it would go, Paul jumped with pain, and the finger was withdrawn with a *pop*.

'All right in that department. You can stand again, and we'll use up what I've put in the syringe. It might stop you catching a cold.'

As the needle went in, the doctor decided to distract Paul. 'What made you think you'd got gonorrhoea in the first place?'

'Well, actually I came to talk to you about something else.'

There was a pause before the doctor's eyes slid down to the syringe in his hand. Then he controlled himself visibly. 'Oh, yes?'

Style was not dead.

'I have this woman living with me. It's really about her. She was assaulted, you see. By some boys. She was lying by the roadside, and they just came along, and ... well, got into her. Now she's pregnant. She was trying to walk to Fleetwood, you see. Where she'd spent her honeymoon.'

The doctor turned away, and dropped the syringe into a pedal-bin, which was covered in red velvet to match the walls.

'It's due on February the fourteenth or thereabouts, but I think she's started to bleed.' The doctor was washing his hands again. The soap looked like marble, and smelled of sandalwood. 'Of course Mary thinks it's her period. She doesn't understand that she can't be pregnant and have periods.'

'You say she hasn't been to a Clinic?'

'I didn't send her because ...'

'Or seen a doctor?'

'No.'

'Then how does she know she's pregnant?'

'She has a ...' Paul gestured with his hands to make the shape of Mary's large belly. 'And once I felt the baby kick.' The doctor turned from the sink, and looked at Paul. 'Well, I think I did. It certainly felt like a kick.' The doctor waited for Paul to continue. 'It was while I was measuring her ...' Again he gestured to make the shape of Mary's belly. The doctor raised one eyebrow; as a boy, he had practised this. 'It was very slight. I suppose it could have been a hiccup.'

'How old is your woman?'

'Forty-five or forty-six, I think.'

'Then, unless she's a very special woman indeed, you can take it from me that she's having you on. One way of making sure, of course, would be to look at her tits. Take a good look at the nipples. If they're enlarged, and brown instead of pink, then bring her back to me, and I'll examine her.'

'Thank you.'

'I'll have to send you a bill, I'm afraid, Paul.'

'Yes, of course.'

'Still, it's always useful to know you haven't got gonorrhoea.'

# MARY'S BABY

The moment the B.B.C. announced that the time was nine a.m., Mary had her first contraction. The date was February the fourteenth, St Valentine's Day, and it was a Saturday.

When Mary told Paul about her first contraction, he remarked that the baby was very punctual, and that this was a good sign. The book said 'Not to Panic', and he had read the book twice, first to himself, and then aloud to Mary, though when reading it to Mary he had missed out all the bits that might have upset her. He was not going to panic under any circumstances.

Paul asked Mary to sit upright in an easy chair and practise her breathing, while he finished washing up the breakfast things. The book's instruction was to act as naturally as possible, for the first contraction might simply be the start of a long wait. Mary breathed as naturally as possible, and Paul washed up as naturally as possible.

With the washing-up cleared away, Paul prepared Richard's bedroom for labour. The bed was stripped, and a large rubber sheet placed underneath the oldest cotton sheet he could find. Extra pillows were borrowed from Paul's own bed. Mary would need these for support. And a large pair of thick woolly socks were spread out on the carpet beside Richard's bed. All women get cold feet when it comes to labour.

Mary placed the tips of her fingers in the arch of her rib cage, and closed her mouth before taking a deep breath through her nose. This breath was her sixty-eighth. If she could have divided sixty-eight by six, she would have known how many half-minutes she had been sitting like this. Her cervix would be getting thinner: the book had said so. Suddenly Mary stopped the controlled breathing, and laughed out loud as she remembered the diagram Paul had shown her. That was what was happening inside her. She was over-excited; the book had said she would be. Her contractions (she had just felt the second) had been so gentle and so short that she wanted something else to happen. Something important. After all, it wasn't every day she had a baby.

With her mouth now open, and her tongue resting loosely against her bottom teeth, Mary sang 'Anyone Who Had A Heart Could Look At Me, And Know That I Love You' silently in her head. Strictly speaking, she should have tapped out a rhythm on her lap or a table, but she was too excited for that. Mary stamped out the rhythm with her feet, moving alternate feet backwards and forwards, and then from side to side, to make a little dance.

At twelve mid-day, Mary came back from the toilet, and reported to Paul that she had had what the book called 'a show'. Paul asked her how much blood she had passed. She replied that it was just enough to colour her water pink.

While she was reporting this progress, Mary pissed on the living-room carpet. At first she was upset, but Paul said 'I expect that's your water breaking, Mary,' and Mary saw that this was so. It was no more than a cup-full, and Paul mopped it up with a cloth before running Mary a hot bath.

Mary sat in Richard's sunken bath, splashing water over herself. The bathroom door was half open, and Paul stood on the other side of it, peeling potatoes. The bath water was hot, and Mary had been afraid that the heat of the water might tell Baby not to come. Paul explained that it was too late for that, and reminded her that the book had recommended hot water. This was not a bath to get Mary clean, but to increase the circulation of blood in her tummy. Mary soaped under her arms and between her legs just the same.

According to Sister Pratt's book, the next thing for Paul to do was to cook Mary a large meal. This he did, but not until she had grown bored with lying in the bath, and was dressing herself in nightie and dressing-gown. When Mary came into the kitchen, Paul handed her a cup of strong sweet tea. Tea no longer made her feel sick. Eggs and bacon were waiting to be fried, while Paul dropped chips, as he cut them, into hot deep fat. The hot fat spat at him, and Mary asked if she could help. Paul shook his head, and told her to think about life. Mary thought about the eggs, bacon and chips. They were her favourite food.

After lunch Paul timed one of Mary's contractions. Since each one lasted no more than three seconds, they could not be described as urgent.

At five p.m., the contractions were still only lasting three seconds. It worried Paul that Mary might decide to have a long and difficult phantom labour, for the book had not given details about how to perform a Caesarean.

At six twenty-five, Paul told Mary that he expected her to start 'Labour Proper' soon.

At six thirty-five, Mary's pains began to last at least two minutes each, and Paul guided her to Richard's bed. The dressing-gown was taken off, and the woolly socks put on, while Mary continued the breathing exercises and singing under her breath. Paul then left the room for a moment, and returned wearing a white overall he had specially bought, and a face-mask he had made out of a large handkerchief. When Mary saw him, she laughed so much and for so long that she lost count of her breaths, and forgot the tune of 'Anyone Who Had a Heart'.

Next Paul brought his razor from the bathroom, and explained that he was supposed to shave off her pubic hair.

He had not read this part of Sister Pratt's book out loud because, he said, he had not wanted to trouble Mary with this problem until it was necessary. Now it was necessary. If she wished verification, he would show her the page he had turned down. Mary asked why she could not do it herself, and Paul said that if she wished to risk crushing the baby by bending her body double he would not be held responsible.

Mary closed her eyes, and lifted her nightie slowly. Paul put the razor down beside the bed, and assisted her legs apart. He apologized for having forgotten to buy ordinary shaving soap, so that he had to squirt on Erasmic Super Foam.

At seven thirty p.m., Paul and Mary sat waiting for the 'Transition Stage'. In this stage, Paul had told her, women either became tired, and wanted to sleep between contractions instead of staying alert as they should, or they became nasty and ill-tempered, and often shouted at anyone close. Paul wondered which sort of woman Mary would choose to be.

At eight fifteen p.m., Paul, who had been sitting watching Mary breathe, stood to leave the room. 'Where are you off to?' Mary said, in a voice which was too loud.

'I thought I'd get a book to read. You won't let the irritability affect your breathing pattern, will you?'

'What do you mean, "irritability"? I asked you a simple bloody question,' Mary screamed at the top of her voice.

'Yes, of course you did. I'm sorry. I'm not supposed to argue with you, or try to make you reasonable.'

'I am reasonable.'

'Of course you are.' Mary sank back on to the bed. She could think of nothing else to shout.

At eight thirty-five, she remembered. 'Where's my bloody sponge?'

'In the bathroom. I'll get it.' Paul left the room, and returned quickly with the small sponge he had bought, following the book's instructions.

'That's a fat lot of good. I should have been sucking it from the start.'

'No, at the very start you had a meal, remember?' Paul attempted to pass the small sponge across Mary's lips.

'Piss off.' Both of them were shocked by Mary's language, and being shocked, they laughed.

At nine twenty-six, Paul reminded Mary what the book had said about pushing. Sister Pratt had stressed that one could never push too late, but that it was dangerous for the baby if the mother tried to push it out too soon. Mary replied that she felt the need to push, so Paul told her that she must wait until he had examined her pelvic floor. Lifting her nightie, he placed two fingers where he had shaved her. Mary closed her eyes. Paul slid his two fingers into Mary's vagina, and moved them gently. Mary gripped the sheet she was lying on. This was another part of the book which Paul had not read out to Mary. He had not read it out, because the book had said that the 'Two-Finger Test' should only be performed by a doctor or midwife.

At nine thirty, Paul removed his fingers and told Mary that she might now lie across the bed, and prepare to push with her next pain. Mary said that she had a tight sensation around her tummy, and Paul reassured her that this was as it should be. After Paul's Two-Finger Test, Mary began to sweat a great deal. Paul wiped her face and neck with the sponge from Timothy White's. He said she must concentrate on her breathing, and sang 'Anyone Who Had a Heart' out loud to remind her of the tune.

By nine thirty-five, Mary was lying across Richard's bed, her back supported by pillows, and her feet resting against Paul's shoulders. The time had come to push. She complained that she had something the size of a tennis ball in her – she could not remember the name for it. Paul told her that the name was 'vagina'.

At nine thirty-seven, Paul began to talk encouragingly to Mary. The book had said that the talk could be about anything the expectant mother might find diverting, so Paul talked to Mary about the stately homes they had visited.

By eleven seven, Mary had been tapping at her thigh, and singing 'Anyone Who Had a Heart' for well over an hour. All this time, she had been pushing at Paul's shoulders with her feet. Paul had run out of conversation several times.

At eleven twenty, Paul said, 'Have you got piles, Mary?'

'Yes.'

'I thought you had. I couldn't help noticing.'

At eleven thirty, Paul told Mary that the baby's head was completely out, and that she could stop pushing. Mary turned over on her right side, and began to pant like a dog.

The phantom baby slid out, and gave a phantom cry. The book had said that this would not be pain, but simply the effect of first contact with this atmosphere. Paul checked inside the phantom baby's mouth for phantom mucus, and found none. Then he cut the phantom umbilical cord in two places. One cut was two inches from Mary, the other two inches from the phantom baby. He wrapped the phantom baby in a blanket, and carried it into the bathroom.

Mary turned over, and with her last contraction, delivered the phantom afterbirth.

Paul stood in the bathroom, in front of the mirror, holding the phantom baby, and wondering what to do. After four minutes' thought, he flushed it down the W.C. Then he poured bleach into the pan, and returned to Richard's bedroom.

Mary was lying with her head turned away, and her eyes closed. As he approached, she held out her right arm for the baby. Paul undid the top three buttons of her nightie, and touched her right breast.

'Does it want food already?'

'Yes.'

'Is it a boy or a girl?'

'It's dead, Mary. I flushed it down the toilet.' Paul lay on Richard's bed beside Mary, his lips to her right breast. After a moment, he began to suck.

Mary felt Paul's tongue and lips sucking at her nipple, and enjoyed the sensation of milk being drawn out. She wondered what Albert would say.

Albert said, 'I'm glad you've found an interest, girl. You see, I lost all mine.'